The Secrets of the Twisted Cross

Case No. 6

A Belltown Mystery

By
T. M. Murphy

J. N. TOWNSEND PUBLISHING
EXETER, NEW HAMPSHIRE
2002

Printed in Canada
Published by J. N. Townsend Publishing
  4 Franklin Street
  Exeter, NH 03833
  603/778-9883
  800/333-9883
  www.jntownsendpublishing.com
  www.belltownmysteries.com

ISBN 1-880158-43-4

Acknowledgments

I would like to thank these loyal Belltown Mystery supporters: Seth Thomas, John Furfey, Mike Forns, Liz Leary, Matt Mann, Dave Watson, Marie Brigham, Alison Birmingham, Beth Surdut, Jim Cox, Alan Hergott, Toni Phillips, Jay Williams, Shannon Murphy, Marsha Malone, Janet McGrath, Amanda Hayes, and Ryder Ferris.

The following people are my out-of-school teachers who have inspired me over the years to write entertaining, but meaningful stories for young people. My profound thanks to Bono, Harper Lee, Horton Foote, Steven Spielberg, George Lucas, Doug Flutie, Elmer Bernstein, John Williams, James Horner, and the late great teachers of fantasy and life—Rod Serling and Joseph Campbell.

For my sisters, Nina, Joanna, Sarah, and Courtney—
Whenever life makes me fall, these four angels have always
picked me up and carried me on their wings.

Chapter
One

BORED. I GUESS that's not the best word to use when beginning a book, but, as you know by now, I'm not writing books. I'm writing firsthand accounts of my cases, and bored is exactly how I felt while looking at furniture with my mom. I wasn't bored because I had spent my whole Sunday with Mom. In fact, I had a great talk with her at lunch. She really seemed to listen while I explained why I keep putting myself into danger—to uncover the truth and to help people. Mom said, "It's a wonderful quality to want to help people. And if law enforcement is what you want to pursue, I promise you, Dad and I will back you a hundred and ten percent. But, for now, Orville, can't you just try to be a normal sixteen-year-old boy?"

I smiled. "I'll try, Mom."

As I thought back on that conversation, I realized after what I had seen and been through in the past few months, there was no way my life would ever be normal again. I knew I would always have to watch my back since Ivan Petralkov, a former KGB agent and professional killer who wanted me dead, was still on the loose. That was something I could never let Mom know about. It was bad enough that I had sleepless nights, but why expose her to that fear—especially since my Dad was still on a teaching exchange in Ireland. So, knowing that the lunatic Ivan Petralkov was still free to seek his revenge made looking at furniture a somewhat mundane experience.

But, I knew if Ivan had any brains, he was probably far, far away from Belltown, Cape Cod. Well, at least that's what I was hoping as I sat in a rocking chair and tested it for Mom.

"Well, Orville, what do you think? Do you like it?"

"Mom, it rocks."

"Boy, that was a lousy pun." Mom smiled.

"You can say that again, Mrs. Jacques." A voice came from behind us. I turned my head and standing behind the counter of the Belltown Hospital Thrift Store was my buddy, Scotty Donovan.

"Orville, get your degree before you hit the comedy circuit." Scotty grinned as he came over to us.

"Thanks for the advice. Scotty, I didn't know you worked here."

"Volunteer is more like it. It was my Dad's idea, since he's a doctor and all."

"What's that have to do with it?"

"Everything here is donated from people who have either died or moved into nursing homes. All the proceeds go to the hospital for research or to care for people who can't afford it. Anyway, everyone in my family volunteers one weekend a month. This weekend, it's me. So, what can I help you with?"

"What a nice thing to do, Scotty," Mom complimented.

Scotty blushed. "It's no big deal, really. But anyway, Mrs. Jacques, have you seen the rocking chairs in the back?" He pointed.

"No."

"Come with me. We have a few nice ones at very reasonable prices."

"Great. Lead the way." She followed.

I reluctantly got out of the chair and was about to follow when I noticed that we were not the only people in the store. There was a man crouched catcher-style in the back room. He was intently inspecting a gray metal trunk with a spyglass like Sherlock Holmes used.

"Scotty." I pointed over at the man. "Is he allowed to be in the back room?"

"No. Excuse me for a second." Scotty walked over to the man. "Sir, I'm sorry but this room is off limits," Scotty said, startling the man who jumped to his feet.

"You scared me, young man," he barked. He was middle-aged, with a pencil-thin mustache.

"I'm sorry, I didn't mean to. I just wanted you to know that this stuff was just donated, and it hasn't been priced yet."

"Well, I was looking to buy this trunk to store some of my manuscripts. How much?" Pencil-thin mustache reached into his coat pocket and pulled out his checkbook.

"I'm sorry, I can't sell it to you until one of the supervisors prices it," Scotty apologized.

"When will that be?"

"Tomorrow."

"Not good enough. I live down Cape and I never get up here much. I'm willing to write a check for a hundred dollars right now. Take it or leave it," the man pushed.

"A hundred bucks for a metal trunk? Why so much?"

"As I alluded to, I'm a writer and someday my original manuscripts will be worth a heck of a lot more than a hundred dollars. I see the metal that makes up this trunk can withstand fire and other poor conditions. That's my reason. I'm also aware that my money goes to charity. Why not pay a few more dollars than this trunk is really worth? Do we have a deal or not?"

Scotty still looked a little unsure, but said, "Ah, OK."

The man scribbled the check and the transaction was over in a flash. As the man walked out of the store, carrying the gray metal trunk, Scotty turned to us before putting the check into the register. "I hope I just did the right thing."

A minute later, the door burst open. It was Dr. Donovan, Scotty's dad.

"Scotty, please tell me that man who just drove away didn't buy anything."

"Yeah, just a metal trunk for his manuscripts. He's a writer. I got a great price. A hundred bucks!"

Dr. Donovan's face dropped. "Son, that was Clark Harrison and he's no writer."

"Well, who is he then?" Scotty asked nervously.

"The premier antiques collector in all of Cape Cod."

"What, Dad?"

"You heard me, son."

"An antiques dealer. But he said… Oh, no!"

No one said another word. No words were needed. Scotty Donovan, trying to be a Good Samaritan, had just been taken. But for how much? All we could do is wonder in silence. What was the real worth of the gray metal trunk? I figured we would probably never know. I figured wrong.

On the ride home, Mom and I entertained each other by giving our own theories of why the gray metal box was so valuable; that is, if it really was valuable at all!

"Orville, that Harrison fellow mentioned how the metal could withstand poor conditions. Maybe that box was made from a combination of compounds that aren't used any more."

"Well, that would probably explain why he was looking at it with a spy glass. But I was kind of hoping for something much more exciting, like maybe Babe Ruth stored his equipment in it or it came from the *Titanic* or something."

"Don't ever lose that wonderful imagination." She smiled and turned the wheel left onto Harbor Avenue.

"Orville, look over there." Mom pointed over to a police cruiser and a minivan parked in front of a summerhouse. I knew exactly who the minivan belonged to: my mentor and friend, Detective Shane O'Connell. A police cruiser and Shane meant only one thing—a crime had been committed. My detective mouth was foaming.

"Mom, could you, ah…"

"You want me to pull over so you can see what Shane's investigating." She frowned.

"Well, ah, yeah. I know we had that great talk and all, but I just want to check it out. Is it OK?"

"I guess it's my fault. I pointed it out." She pulled in behind Shane's minivan.

"If he lets you stay with him, just give me a wave."

"Thanks, Mom. You're the best." I gave her a peck on the cheek and jumped out. Shane was beside the van.

"That man's boat was stolen."

"When?" I asked.

"We don't know. He summers here and checks on the house once every couple of months. Don't say a word. Just watch." Shane walked back into the garage, and I followed. Officer Jameson and I exchanged what's-up nods and listened to Shane.

"Mr. Mills, I just have a couple of questions and then I think we'll be through."

"Yes, anything Detective. But who's the kid? Did he see anything? Did he see who stole my boat?" Mr. Mills looked at me hopefully.

"No. I have to talk to that young man concerning some shop-lifting incidents." I could tell Officer Jameson was trying not to laugh at Shane's cover.

"Now, anyway, I want to go over this one more time because I want all the facts to be accurate for your insurance company. The boat is insured?" Shane flicked on his pen.

"Of course, Detective."

Shane looked down at his pad. "OK. It was an eighteen-foot Boston Whaler and you stored it in this garage in the winter."

"Yes, Detective. This was the first winter I kept it down

here. I was sick of lugging it all the way up to my house in New Hampshire, so I put it in the garage Labor Day weekend."

"That makes sense," Shane said, while writing it down. Suddenly, he jerked his head up and scanned the garage. All three of us watched him as he walked over to a workbench that had all sorts of tools. Finally, he stopped. He found what he was looking for—a tape measure.

"Orville, give me a hand. Hold onto this and stand at the edge of the garage."

I did as Shane asked, while he held onto the end of the measuring tape and went to the back of the garage.

"What are you doing?" Mr. Mills asked nervously.

"One second, Mr. Mills. Orville, what does the tape measure read?"

I looked down, "Fifteen feet, eight inches."

"Thanks," Shane released the measuring tape and it spun back into the silver holder in my hand.

"Mr. Mills, I am dying to hear how you were able to fit your eighteen-foot Boston Whaler into a fifteen-foot, eight-inch garage. How were you able to do that, sir?"

There was a pained expression on Mr. Mills' face.

"How much were you going to collect from your insurance company?"

"I want my lawyer now, Detective." Mr. Mills was defeated.

"You beat me to the punch. I'm supposed to arrest you first. Officer Jameson, you can do the honors."

"I would be happy to, Detective O'Connell." Officer Jameson cuffed Mr. Mills, told him his rights, and then escorted him into the cruiser.

"Shane, that was awesome! I had no idea he would have stolen his own boat." I was impressed.

"You're not the only one who solves crimes in this town."

"But why did he do it?" I was a little confused.

"This is probably not the first time he pulled a scam like this. You see, I figure he sold the boat in another country so it would be hard to trace and wanted to cash in on the insurance money. Double his pleasure. We'll need a confession out of him or more proof to make it stick. But, Mills isn't the smartest guy I've ever dealt with. He'll talk. Speaking of talking, I'll ask Jameson to handle it because we have something to talk about." Shane turned and headed for the cruiser.

"What do we have to talk about?"

Shane turned around and faced me. "What would you say if I told you that I might have a case that is right up your alley?"

"I'd say," I paused and then laughed, "where's the alley and when do I start?"

Hugh, the owner of Coffee Obsession, poured Shane another cup and then looked around the empty café and shook his head. "Slow night, huh, Hugh?" I asked.

"Yeah. I need some reggae to lift my spirits." Hugh went behind the counter and put on a CD. A second later, the smiling voice of Bob Marley warmed "Coffee O."

"So, when are you going to tell me why I'm here?" I asked Shane while sipping my second hot chocolate.

He looked down at his watch. "You'll know soon enough. Just enjoy your cup."

"I still can't believe that Mills guy," I said. That was pretty cool how you figured that one out."

"There's nothing cool about it." Shane took a gulp from his cup.

"What do you mean?"

"I mean, I almost believed his story. Mills almost cashed in on my poor detective work. Orville, if you want to be in this investigating business for a long time, remember a few things," he said, while rubbing his mustache with his forefinger.

I leaned over. "Yeah, what?"

"Always listen to what a person says, but not just here," Shane pointed to his left ear.

"Then where?"

Shane pointed to his eyes, his forehead and then he tapped his finger on his heart. "Always listen with your eyes, your head, and your gut, because that's what's *really* talking. I almost forgot that today."

The bell above the door jingled, interrupting our conversation. Like everything Shane has ever told me, I quickly registered it into my mental bank for a later withdrawal. A man in his fifties with a black beard, carrying a briefcase, came over to our table. He looked familiar, but I couldn't place him. Hugh popped his head out from behind the counter. "Rabbi Spielman, what can I get you?"

I know I've met him somewhere, I thought.

Rabbi Spielman smiled. "Hugh, in view of the music, how about a medium Jamaican blend."

Hugh laughed. "Coming right up."

The Rabbi and Shane exchanged greetings while shaking hands. "This is Orville Jacques," Shane said as I put out my hand.

"Orville and I have actually met before at Gina Goldman's birthday party last year. Gina's a great kid, except for her love of disco music. I'll take Marley over the Bee Gees any day." Rabbi Spielman smiled as Hugh handed him his cup of Jamaican Java.

"You can say that again." I toasted him with my cup before we all settled into our chairs.

Shane gave us a serious look and then said, "Before we go any further, I just want it on record that I'm not here as a detective from the Belltown Police Department. I'm here as a mutual friend. And as a friend of both of you, I see you both have a problem."

"What are you talking about? I don't have any problems." I stared at Shane.

"In a minute I will leave and the Rabbi will explain his problem, which I feel, Orville, you are more than qualified to help him with. As for your problem, it's investigating. You can't seem to stop, and it's going to get you killed if you don't watch out. Hopefully, this case will let you investigate but won't be dangerous. If it becomes dangerous, you come to me. Other than that, I don't know anything about this." Before I could nod, Shane got up and the bell jingled his exit. I totally understood where Shane was coming from. He had stuck his neck out for me on more than one occasion when it came to cases I worked on. If it got out that he was now throwing cases to the teenage sleuth, he would not just get into hot water, he'd probably lose his job!

"OK, Rabbi Spielman, what can I help you with?"

The Rabbi reached into his briefcase and pulled out a

white manila folder and pushed it across the table. I opened the folder and saw a stack of photos. The first one was of a red Nazi swastika painted on a doorway.

"That's the front of my house," he said.

I nodded and studied the second one. It was even more repulsive—spray painted on a garage was "Go away Jews" and "Hittler Rules."

"That one happened a week later. It was my neighbor's garage that time."

I stopped for a second. "In this picture Hitler is spelled with two T's. I thought he only had one T in his name."

"Exactly. That's how ignorant this person or persons are. That is usually the case with people who commit hate crimes. They don't have the education or the knowledge to know exactly what they're doing, and the history that is really behind those painful words and symbols. They are just wounded animals who need some outlet to attack. I feel sorry for them. I really do." Rabbi Spielman's voice was sincere. There was a sadness to it. I flipped through the ten other similar photos and then put them back into the folder and handed it back to Rabbi Spielman.

"So, I take it you want me to find out who's committing these hate crimes?" I asked.

"Yes."

"How long has this been going on?"

"The first incident was this summer. And then there was one every couple of weeks. But now, it seems to happen every couple of nights."

"I don't get it. Why hasn't it been in the paper? I would think you would want to publicize this hate and not sweep it under the rug."

"That's a good point, Orville, and that is usually common practice among my people when we are faced with anti-Semitism. But, I felt I should take a different approach on this one." Rabbi Spielman put the folder back into his briefcase.

"Why?"

"For the most part, Belltown is a wonderful place filled with different ethnic backgrounds who all get along. Forty of my fifty-five years I've lived here. Not one problem. So why taint the image of this town because of a few ignorant people? And that's exactly what they want. Attention. I don't want to give it to them before I have to. Believe me, my decision was very controversial with the other victims. Orville, will you take our case?"

I was a bit shocked that he had put his faith in me. "Why isn't Detective O'Connell investigating it?"

"He is, but he thinks you can find out more on your end."

"My end? What do you mean?"

"We both feel whoever is committing these crimes is a teenager or teenagers. We think that they probably go to Belltown High. It is my hope that you can find out who is doing this, and I can step in and educate them before they ruin not only the image of Belltown, but themselves."

"I can't believe you'd actually want to help these people." I was trying to make sense out of it all.

"Orville, a child isn't born with hate. A child is taught. I want to reeducate this young person or people who can't even spell out their hate that there is a better way. Well, Orville, can I count on you to help?"

"Yes, but I'll need those pictures."

He reached back into his briefcase and handed me the folder.

"I won't tell the other victims that you're working on the case considering, well, y'know."

"My age." I said it for him. I understood. They probably would think that their case wasn't being taken seriously if they knew a teenager was working on it.

"But I will call them tonight and tell them someone will begin working on their case tomorrow."

"But, I'm not starting tomorrow."

"Oh, well, when will you start?" Rabbi Spielman looked curious.

I looked at him straight in the eye and said, "Ten minutes ago. Now tell me about the other victims."

CHAPTER
TWO

I REALLY WASN'T trying to sound dramatic when I told the Rabbi that I started working on the case ten minutes ago. It was the truth. The minute he gave me his theory that a student from Belltown High might be involved in the hate crimes, my mind began to race with the question, Who could it be? It was a question I couldn't answer. That question vibrated against my brain the following day when everyone gathered in the gym for a pep rally for the hockey team. I sat beside Gina, contemplating letting her in on the case. I knew, as in the past, her expertise with her computer might be helpful down the line, that is, if there was a down the line. "This pep rally should be pretty lame, but at least we have a free period. You can't beat that," I smiled.

"Yeah, whatever." Gina gave me a monotone response.

That exchange told me that Gina wasn't her cheerful

self. Most of the time "whatever" to my friends and me meant drop the subject or stop talking, I'm not interested. But then there were the times that "whatever" meant something is bothering me. I knew this was one of those times and decided not to tell her about the case.

I quizzed her. "Ace, what's the deal? You don't seem yourself."

"Can you please stop calling me by that stupid nickname!" She glared at me and then turned away.

"Well, now I know something's wrong 'cause you love that nickname. C'mon, Gina, what's wrong?"

"Everything, Orville. Here's yours." Gina handed me an envelope with my name on it. I opened it and began to read the card out loud. "You are cordially invited to a surprise party celebrating Vanessa Hyde's sixteenth birthday."

Gina interrupted. "I saw Mr. Hyde at the post office the other day and he asked me to give it to you."

"I don't understand, Gina. You're not jealous 'cause I got invited and you didn't?" I didn't understand why she would be upset. After all, Vanessa and I were kind of seeing each other.

"No, Mr. Hyde invited me, too."

"Oh, OK." I paused. She wasn't helping me. "Wait, Gina, you're not, ah, jealous of Vanessa and me?"

Gina burst into a fit of laughter for about a minute.

"Oh, man, Orville. Jealous. Wow. You always know how to cheer me up." Gina was still giggling.

I was getting annoyed. "OK, you're not jealous. Let's stop the guessing games. I've got more important stuff to think about."

"I'm sorry, Orville, my emotions are all over the place these days, and it's because of Dan." She was referring to Dan "Franco" Francais, one of my best friends whom Gina had been dating for a few days.

"Why? What's up with you and Franco?"

Gina was serious again. "I asked him if he wanted to go to Vanessa's party as my date and he said we had to talk."

"And?"

"We talked. He said it wasn't working out. He gave me the old 'I-think-we-should-be-friends' line. And how he had to concentrate on his studies."

I couldn't help but laugh. "What kind of line is that? This is high school, not law school."

"I know. I told him how weak it was to end it with a lame excuse like that. Anyway, that's why I'm in such a bad mood." Gina ended our conversation as Mr. Finn, the principal of Belltown High, grabbed the microphone.

"Could everyone please settle down so we can get the rally started?" He motioned for quiet and after a couple of seconds he was satisfied to continue.

"Great, thank you all for coming."

"Like we had a choice," I whispered to Gina.

"It's not often that we have the entire student body in one place, so before we begin the rally I'd like to inform you all of a new rule that will be in effect next week."

There was a loud groan.

"OK, OK. Calm down. It is nothing big. It is just a hat ban. Now no one will be allowed to wear a hat during the entire school day or they'll receive a detention."

"What!"

"You gotta be kidding!"

"No way!"

"I hate this school!"

These were a few of the comments angry students blurted out. I was one of them because on those days when I woke up and had bed-head and only ten minutes to make the bus, a baseball hat was my savior. Mr. Finn didn't realize it, but he had just altered hundreds of students' sleeping schedules. He scanned the crowd and realized his timing was poor.

"I guess I shouldn't have brought this up now. Why don't we get the rally started?"

"What about the Cohen brothers?" Paul Miller shouted out. "Does that mean they can't wear their hats anymore?"

"Paul, they're yarmulkes, not hats. And yes, David and Barry can still wear them."

"Those things are like hats. They cover the back of their heads." Miller's face turned red as he protested.

"Yes, but David and Barry are Jewish and wearing the yarmulke is part of their religion." Mr. Finn's tone was, Drop it, Miller.

"Well, my religion is the Red Sox and this is my way of worshipping them!" Miller pointed to his hat and got a few laughs from the wise guys in the crowd. Mr. Finn just rolled his eyes and continued on to introduce the band. As the band marched out playing the Belltown fight song, I wondered about Paul Miller's anger. Was he a suspect? Could it be that easy? He definitely fit the profile: he was ignorant and angry. I had witnessed both of these characteristics the week before when he and Craig Hampton picked on Larry, a homeless man. I was definitely going to keep my eye on Paul Miller.

My train of thought was broken when I heard laughter above the band music. I looked over at the gym door and spotted the hockey team walking through the gym entrance. Each player had his jersey on and was waving his we-are-number-one finger. Each player also had one other thing which was the source of the laughter—a buzz cut. From Coach Forbes to the quiet equipment manager, Matt Dunn, every head was shaved to the scalp. At that moment, I was thankful that baseball was my sport!

I chomped on my slice of soggy cafeteria pizza, trying to figure out a game plan for my case, as the rest of the table struggled with the challenging topics of life.

"How can you say *Jaws* isn't one of the best movies of all time?" Scotty Donovan argued with Sean Driscoll.

"I didn't say that I didn't love *Jaws*. It's a classic. What I'm saying is that the *Jaws* series of movies got a little out of hand."

"What do you mean, Sean?" my friend, Christa Soderstrom, asked.

"It gets pathetic by the last movie. The Great White shark now has a vendetta against this one woman and her family so she finally has the sense to move from Martha's Vineyard, but where does she move? Does she move to Idaho where there are no oceans filled with sharks? No. The mother decides to escape from the shark by moving to a tropical island." Sean put his hands up in the air in mock disgust, and the table broke into laughter. "But wait. What's even worse is the *same* shark follows her all the way from the Vineyard to the tropical island." Sean smiled and folded his arms.

Scotty grinned and admitted, "Yeah, that is pretty pathetic."

"That's like that show 'Murder, She Wrote.' Have you ever seen reruns of that?" Christa didn't wait for an answer as she continued. "This woman named Jessica Fletcher solves cases. It's pretty good but wherever this woman goes someone always ends up murdered. I'll tell you one thing, watch your back if she shows up at your house for dinner. I'd have a complex if I were her." Christa's serious tone caused everyone to laugh more.

"With the luck Orville has had finding dead bodies that must mean he must have a complex," Scotty added. But the laughter sputtered and then stopped. It seemed that everyone was seriously considering my bad luck at stumbling into danger.

"Sorry, Orville. Just kidding." Scotty shrugged.

"No problem, Scotty." In all of this joking around, Scotty had made a point I had never considered. Did I have bad luck? As I reflected on my past adventures, Scotty spent the next five minutes telling the group about Clark Harrison, the antiques dealer, and how he had played him for a fool.

The group loved how honest Scotty was about being taken. I wasn't paying much attention to his story until he came to a part that I hadn't witnessed.

"So, I'm closing the store with my Dad and I'm feeling like a complete idiot when the phone rings. I pick it up and the voice on the other end asks if anyone dropped off a gray metal trunk. I go on to tell him it has already been sold. He freaks out, asking questions like: When was it sold, who bought it? Stuff like that. I fell for it for a minute or so, until I realized it's Orville disguising his voice."

The bell sounded ending Scotty's story.

"Ah, that's cold, Orville, rubbing it in like that," Sean Driscoll shook his head.

"Scotty, what are you talking about? I didn't call you last night." I was shocked.

Scotty laughed. "Yeah, whatever, Orville. I gotta get to class. Hey, I'll give you credit, you almost had me. Later."

Scotty tossed his empty milk carton into the trash and dashed up the stairs. As much as I wanted to concentrate on my own case, I was thinking of the ordinary-looking gray, metal trunk and what made it so *unordinary*.

When the school day ended, my plan was to go home and call Shane. I was going to inform him about Paul Miller's comments and then ask him for some guidance in my investigation. I really didn't know how to start. My plan had to wait when I suddenly remembered that I had Driver's Education class. I sprinted outside and saw Dan "Franco" Francais starting to pull out of the high school parking lot. I knew I would make it because Franco wasn't the fastest driver around. I caught up to the gold Toyota Camry in no time, and tapped on the back passenger window. Franco, who was breaking the turtle sound barrier at a whopping five miles an hour, slammed on the brakes, making the two passengers do a snap-back movement. Matt Dunn opened the back door and I stumbled in.

"Sorry I'm late, Miss Turner. I got caught up studying my hand signals," I smiled.

"That's OK, Orville. I'm just glad you're here because the sooner you get your driving done, the sooner you get your license, and the sooner you get your license, the sooner you get your freedom." Miss Turner smiled. That's why every student loved her. Miss Turner could totally relate to us. Maybe part of the reason she could was being in her mid-twenties, so she still remembered what the teenage years were like. Miss Turner had been teaching Spanish and Drivers Ed. in Belltown for two years, and she already had a yearbook dedicated to her. That didn't exactly make her popular with the faculty, though, because some of them lived for that kind of stuff. Mr. Reasons, my hated algebra teacher, was once heard saying, "She only got it dedicated to her because all of the boys have a crush on her."

That was one of the few times I agreed with unreasonable Reasons. Every guy at Belltown High did have a crush on her, and I was no exception!

"Dan, why don't you take a right at the stop sign and head for Breakers Beach." She pointed with one of her long, painted red fingernails and Franco spun the wheel.

"Orville, when we get to Breakers Beach, you can take over," she said over her shoulder.

"What about Matt? Shouldn't he go next?" I offered.

"Scared, Orville?" Franco looked at me in the rearview mirror.

"No, not at all. It's just that I thought the last one in the car is the last one to drive."

"Normally, you'd be right. But it's easier this way. My apartment is right by the ice arena and Matt has to go there and get the equipment ready for tonight's game. We can get your driving over and then drop you guys off. Now Dan, please, give it a little more gas," Miss Turner pleaded.

"Yeah, Franco. You might pass that kid riding his bike with the training wheels," I joked and Miss Turner laughed.

"Very funny, Orville." Franco frowned up into the mirror.

"OK, now Dan take a left up here."

"But, Miss Turner, I thought we were going to Breakers Beach?" He hesitated.

"We are. This is a shortcut."

"Are you sure?" I asked.

"Believe me, I'm a Driver's Ed. teacher. I have to know every road and back road in this town."

Franco took the turn and went from side road to side road for about ten minutes while I tried to talk to Matt Dunn. *Tried* was the operative word. Ever since Matt moved to Belltown in the fifth grade, the kid hadn't talked.

"So, Matt, are we going to have a good hockey team this year?"

He looked at me almost shocked that I was attempting to talk to him. Finally, he said, "I guess so."

"Well, I mean, since you see them play every day, you must have a good idea how they'll do." I tried to help him.

"No. I just help get their stuff ready on game day. Nate Hill is their everyday equipment manager."

"Well, that must be kind of fun, though, being on the bench during the games." Why was I bothering? I wondered.

"I'd rather be playing, but my health and all," he said and looked away. I didn't bother to ask Matt why he didn't try out for the team. Anyone who knew Matt Dunn knew he could never play hockey because of the countless health problems that he had over the years, including two major organ transplants.

"Yeah, Matt. Speaking of health, in bio today, Mrs. Ramone told us about the organ transplant law or rule or whatever you want to call it. Orville, have you heard of it?" Franco jumped into our conversation while Miss Turner began to paint her nails.

"No, what about it?" I asked.

"Well, just that if you receive an organ transplant you can't meet the family of the donor unless you write a letter to the hospital, and I guess then the hospital gives the family the letter. Then if they want to meet you, it's OK. Anyway, Mrs. Ramone said Matt wrote a letter a while back and he's waiting to hear."

"Yeah, so what is your point, Dan?" Matt was agitated.

"My point is, what will you say to the family if you meet them?"

"'Thank you.' What else? They saved my life. Anyway, it was my mother's idea. Can we drop it?"

Franco looked curiously at Matt through the rearview mirror for a minute.

"Watch out!" I yelled and Franco slammed on the brakes, barely avoiding two sea gulls having their shellfish lunch on the beach road.

"I should have known better than to paint my nails," Miss Turner said, while looking at the red polish stain on her pants. "Orville, why don't you take over now."

Franco pulled over to the side of the road and put the car in park. He hopped out of his side and I hopped out of mine. As I passed him in front of the car I asked, "Hey what's up with you and Gina?"

He squinted. "I don't want to talk about it. She just thought it was something more than it really was."

"But, Franco, you really liked …"

Franco jumped into the car and slammed the door. That was strange, I thought. Franco always told me everything. I got back into the car and Miss Turner gave me some brief instructions. I put the car into drive, flicked the blinker, and pulled back onto the road. Miss Turner looked at her watch and then switched on the radio. I gave a quick glance at her because her one rule was never listen to the radio during Driver's Ed. She must've caught the glance because she said, "I want to hear the local news."

I drove along past Breakers Beach. I was going slightly below the speed limit and was pretty proud of my driving as the DJ came on. "Now our top story. As we reported first here at noon, the Silver Shore Police Department found the body of Clark Harrison…"

Clark Harrison! My mind screamed and I hit the brakes and screeched to a stop.

"What the…" Franco and Matt began.

"Ssssh! Quiet!" Miss Turner and I said in unison.

"Mr. Harrison's body was discovered around six o'clock this morning. The Silver Shore Police Department isn't disclosing any more information at this time, but sources tell us foul play could be a factor. Mr. Harrison was a famous antiques collector and dealer for twenty years on the Cape. We will provide you with more information as soon as it is available, so stay tuned. In other news, the bridge repairs on Green Harbor ..." I turned off the radio and was stunned. "What's the matter, Orville? Did you know him?" Miss Turner asked.

I tried to answer her questions but all I could mutter to myself was, "Foul play could be a factor." I didn't have to speculate. I knew what the DJ would report later: "Foul play is a factor." The question was, the gray metal trunk—was that the major factor? I had to find out!

I had to call Shane, I thought, as I thanked Miss Turner and scrambled out of the gold Camry. A wide-eyed Scotty Donovan stood in my front yard blowing on his hands. The expression on his face told me he had heard about Harrison.

"Orville, I've got some news ..." he began.

"I know. Clark Harrison is dead. I just heard it on the radio. Let's go into my Shack and warm up by the wood stove. I've got to ask you something." I lead Scotty over to my renovated garage beside the house where my parents lived. We walked into The Shack and I was thankful to see Mom had built me a fire in the stove.

"Before you ask your question, Orville, I have one." Scotty rubbed his hands in front of the stove.

"I think I know what it is. Shoot."

"In the cafeteria today, you said you weren't the one who made the prank call to me about the metal trunk. Is. . .?

"Yeah, Scotty, it's true. I swear to you, I didn't call you."

Scotty looked straight ahead. "Oh, no. What if I.... They said it might be murder. Orville, could it just be a coincidence? Do you think …" He didn't have the strength to finish.

"Do I think this trunk has something to do with this guy's death? I really don't know. It probably is just a coincidence. Let's not jump the gun here. From your reaction, Scotty, I probably don't have to ask my question but I will anyway. Did you tell the angry guy who called that Clark Harrison had bought the trunk?"

Scotty didn't say a word for a minute. "Yeah. I said his name and that's when I thought it was you rubbing it in. Oh, man, did I help kill him?"

"Slow down, Scotty. That trunk probably has nothing to do with it. We're putting one and one together and we're getting five. We first have to establish two facts. One, if it was murder, and two, if the trunk is missing. This could all be our imaginations running wild."

"OK, well, how are we going to find those things out?"

I thought of my original plan and said, "It's as easy as picking up the phone."

I told Scotty I had to kick him out of The Shack because I had to call my secret source. He was a little reluctant to go until I promised to call the moment I got some information about Clark Harrison's death. The truth is, if I were calling Shane, a.k.a. my secret source, solely to find out about Harrison's death I would have no problem letting Scotty stay.

But, I still had to talk to Shane about my own case. Rabbi Spielman had counted on me and I wasn't going to let him down. I needed Shane's advice and then, hopefully, I could get my investigation of the hate crimes kick-started. Shane listened intently as I described Paul Miller's anger about the Cohen brothers being able to wear their yarmulkes.

"He could be your guy, Orville, or he could just have a stupid sense of humor. There isn't much there to go on."

"So, what do I do?"

"Can you befriend this Miller kid?"

"I doubt it. We've been enemies for awhile."

"Well, at least tell him you agree with him. Make a big issue about the hat ban and the Cohen brothers' yarmulkes in a class."

"But what Miller said was stupid." I was confused.

"Of course, but how are you going to find out who's running around town defacing these good peoples' homes if you make your real feelings known? It's called undercover work. If you make a big deal about it in one of your classes, word will get out that Orville Jacques doesn't think it's fair that the Jewish kids get to wear their yarmulkes, and he can't wear his baseball hat. Then maybe, whoever is running around with the spray can might think you're anti-Semitic, too. Then he, she, or they might ask you to join them."

"Shane, that's brilliant."

"OK, well, I gotta get some dinner. Give me ... "

"Shane, one other thing. How are your relations with the Silver Shore Police Department?"

"Pretty good. I have a few buddies on their force. Why?" He sounded puzzled.

"Because I need a favor."

Shane hadn't heard about Clark Harrison's death so I filled him in on every detail. He was more than interested and said he'd make a few phone calls down Cape and get back to me. I had dinner, did most of my homework, and was about to go to bed when the phone rang. It was Shane.

"I called one of my buddies and he searched everywhere—Harrison's house and store. And guess what, there was no sign of any gray metal trunks. He's going to want to talk to you and your friend Scotty. Especially Scotty, since he was the one who talked to the angry guy on the phone."

"So, I take it then, Harrison was murdered?"

"Yeah, unless he was playing with one of his collectible Civil War swords and suddenly slipped, driving it through his heart," Shane said grimly.

"Oh, man. How… horrible…" I stammered.

My friend Frankie said since nothing else was missing from Harrison's house and the antiques store, that the trunk and the angry caller could be legitimate leads. Good work, Orville, to follow up on your instincts."

I finally recovered. "Thanks. I promised Scotty I'd call him if I had any info. Should I?"

"That's a promise I wouldn't keep. He'll have to deal with it tomorrow. You might as well let him have a good night's sleep. You have a good one, too. Bye."

Click.

"Easy for him," I muttered as I hung up the phone and fell onto my bed.

As I tossed and turned in bed, I knew Scotty was probably sound asleep. "Some people have all the luck," I said to myself, and then thought of what Scotty had said at lunch about my luck. What luck exactly did I have? Only time would tell.

CHAPTER THREE

THE FIRST YAWN finally came around three in the morning, but my heavy brain was still tumbling with visions and thoughts—Paul Miller, spray cans, hate crimes. How could I befriend him? Another yawn brought an even more horrific picture—a Civil War sword stuck in Clark Harrison's chest, the missing trunk, and who killed him? The final yawn brought a better sight—Vanessa Hyde's deep blue eyes smiling into mine at her birthday party. What would be the perfect gift to give her? My eyelids fluttered and fell. Finally, sleep.

"Hello, my little mouse," the voice whispered. I couldn't see the face. It was just a shadow silhouetted by the moonlight. But I didn't have to see the face. I knew. IVAN. Fear swept over me instantly. Ivan Petralkov had come back to finish what he started. He was going to kill me. I lunged from my bed, but his hands surrounded my neck and his claws dug in. He squeezed and hissed laughter as I gagged and flailed, trying hopelessly to save myself. It was no use. I felt the wave of death coming. The end was seconds away.

Ivan giggled like a child. "I will always be with you, Orville. Remember, I am the cat and you are my little mouse. My little mouse. My little mouse...."

I was blacking out waiting to hear the last sounds of the world—my neck being snapped. Then suddenly, the black night was replaced with the morning's winter sun spilling into my room. The clock radio voices shouted traffic reports while I tried to make sense of the situation. I looked down and my sheets were drenched, my bed was a pool of sweat. I shook my head. "Another bad dream."

I thought again of Ivan's grip on my neck and corrected myself. "Nightmare."

Mom once told me, "Always analyze your dreams, Orville. It's your unconscious speaking to you, trying to tell you something important."

I didn't have to analyze this dream. It was telling me, until Ivan Petralkov was caught, he would always be with me. It was a thought that made me never want to sleep again.

I went into my bathroom, turned on the faucet, and threw some water on my face. I glanced into the mirror and noticed I had a strange red rash around the base of my neck. It almost resembled a handprint. I felt my neck and it was sore. For a moment, I ran with the thought, but then I stopped it. No. It was just a nightmare. Yeah, it had to be.

When I got to school, I tried to put Ivan out of my head and refocus my energy back on the hate crime case. I thought Shane gave me some great advice except for the part about befriending Paul Miller. I would have no problem faking friendship with him for the good of the cause, but I knew Miller would never buy it. We had been enemies ever since he threw my glasses out the window of the school bus in the fourth grade. We had too much history to suddenly become buddies. But, speaking of history, I thought that was the perfect place to hatch my plan. History class was the only class Paul Miller and I had together. Mr. Kapulka, who was our sub while our teacher was on maternity leave, clapped his hands enthusiastically. "Everyone file in so we can begin history ..." he stopped and smiled at a group of girls, "and *her*story class."

A few people wrestled in their seats for a minute but then there was silence. Mr. Kapulka was respected by our class. No one ever gave him a hard time, which was pretty rare when it came to substitute teachers in our school. I think part of the reason was he was in his early seventies, and we all considered him to be a grandfather-type figure. Also, we had no clue why this man would want to put up with pimple-faced teenagers all day. But, for some reason he did, and we liked him for that. The other reason we liked him during his brief two month stint in Belltown, was that he didn't just lecture to us. He listened. He was genuinely curious about our views on the world. I knew this was the best class to try my undercover work.

Mr. Kapulka opened the class with his standard line: "Does anyone have anything on his or her mind?"

His eyes moved up and down each row until they found my raised hand. "Yes, Orville. What's on your mind?"

Gina, who was sitting next to me, gave me a curious glance. It wasn't everyday I raised my hand in class. Gina! Gina is Jewish, I thought, and what I'm about to say is really going to upset her. I should have told her about my plan, I scolded myself. "Orville, go ahead. The floor is yours." Mr. Kapulka motioned with his chalk.

There was no turning back. I have to think of the greater good, I rationalized.

"Thank you, Mr. Kapulka. I just wanted everyone to know that I totally disagree with Mr. Finn's decision to outlaw hats in this school. It is completely unfair. He didn't even ask for our input. Don't we count at all?"

"Right on."

"Me too!"

"You said it!"

A few voices agreed.

"So, how would you solve this problem, Orville?" Mr. Kapulka asked.

"I have already thought of a way. I am starting a petition and when it is signed by the students, I am going to bring it to the school committee."

"All right, good for you, man," a voice said.

"I'll sign it," a group of voices followed.

I trembled a bit because what I was about to say was not what I believed, but I had to remember this act would give me the cover I needed to continue investigating the crimes. "I will be taking signatures at lunch today. I feel if those Jewish kids can wear their silly hats, why can't we wear our baseball hats? And, if the school committee decides we still can't wear our hats, then *they* shouldn't be able to wear those ridiculous yarmulkes." I banged my hand on the desk for dramatics. All the "Yeah, I agree" and smiles of unity changed to looks of puzzlement and, for a minute, there was silence.

"Orville, I can't believe you said that. You didn't mean that!" My friend, Wayne Rose, gave me a look of please-explain-yourself. I could feel all their eyes, especially Gina's; hers were filled with confusion.

"It's just that Paul Miller made me think when he made his joke yesterday. Why should those people get special treatment?"

The eyes darted over to Miller. "I didn't say that! I was just joking around that the Red Sox was my religion! I didn't mean that the Cohen brothers shouldn't be able to wear their yarmulkes."

Gina overcame her shock enough to talk. "I can't believe what I'm hearing. Special treatment! Do you know what we had to overcome? Tell him, Mr. Kapulka."

Mr. Kapulka didn't know how to respond.

"OK, if you won't tell him, I will!"

Sue Edward, who was to Gina what Paul Miller was to me, butted in. "Please spare us that Holocaust garbage."

Gina swung her head back. "What did you say?"

Sue said in a bored voice, "Spare us that Holocaust garbage. I heard most of it was made up anyway."

"Made up?!" I thought Gina was going to burst.

Wayne jumped in. "Next you're going to say that there was no slavery."

"Whatever." Sue rolled her eyes.

"Don't whatever me!"

"OK, OK, let's calm down here," Mr. Kapulka pleaded. "Emotions are too high right now to talk about this subject rationally."

"There's nothing to talk about, Mr. Kapulka. Jacques and Edward are bigots." Wayne pointed at Sue and then me.

"Look, for homework I want all of you to begin researching for a paper that will be due at the end of the week. The topic will be 'Was there a Holocaust?'"

"That's absurd. Of course there was." Gina's face was flushed.

"Well, Gina, as we saw here today, not everyone shares your belief. I am going to let class out early today so everyone can cool down." Mr. Kapulka motioned to the door. People didn't jump out of their seats like a normal early dismissal. They walked in a trance. They couldn't believe what had just taken place. I couldn't either!

Sue Edward walked over to me. "I thought that was great what you said."

I didn't know what to say. "Oh, ah, yeah. Thanks."

Wayne interrupted. "Jacques." It was then I noticed that I was no longer Orville to Wayne. "I always knew she was a racist the way she talked about me, and how she treats Gina. But you? You were my friend. How could you?"

Sue snapped her gum. "Why don't you leave us alone?"

Wayne turned to Gina who was nearby, "Gina, let's leave these ignorant fools alone. They're not worth it."

Gina's eyes could've drilled holes in my head. "Yeah, you're right, Wayne. *He's* not worth it."

I watched for a minute as they walked down the hall together. "Don't mind them. Those types of people all stick together. Back to what I was saying. I liked what you were saying, and maybe we can get together sometime." Sue smiled.

"Yeah, that would be great." I smiled back but inside I felt like I was going to be sick. My plan had worked. I had to open up this can of worms to find a second suspect, Sue Edward. My problem was, though, if I didn't prove it was Paul Miller, Sue Edward, or whoever, that can I opened would prove just one thing—I was the biggest worm of them all.

If I wanted the perfect cover, by lunchtime I had it! Word had spread like wildfire throughout the school that I was anti-Semitic. My usual group of friends sat at our table coldly staring across the cafeteria at me while I asked people to sign my petition. I felt extremely guilty because normally that table echoed with laughter while they discussed mindless topics. There was nothing mindless about the topic they were chatting about—a good friend might not be the person they thought he was. I had mixed feelings about their stares. Part of me wanted to yell at them, especially at Gina, for being so quick to believe that I was capable of really harboring those ignorant feelings. But, I said what I said. How were they to know that I was working undercover for Rabbi Spielman? So, the other part of me felt relief for having friends who stuck together and shared the same values. It seemed that was also the case when it came to the majority of the students at

Belltown High—hardly anyone would sign my petition, and the few who did sign it hadn't heard about my hateful words in history class because a few minutes later they returned and fiercely scratched their names off the list. The bell was about to sound when Franco came over to me. At that point, I realized he hadn't been sitting at our table. I figured he probably was going to stay away from the table until Gina cooled down over their break-up. I was a little uneasy as he approached because he knew me well, and would probably see right through my fake attitude.

"Orville, I need to ask you a favor. Can you tell Miss Turner that something came up and I can't make Driver's Ed. today?"

"Yeah, no problem. Why can't you go?" I was surprised he was so civil, considering…

"I'm just tired. I was up pretty late last night. But, tell her I'm sick or something."

"OK," I said as I was about to put my petition notebook into my backpack.

"Don't put that away. I gotta sign it."

"Oh … OK." I was stunned, but I figured he probably hadn't heard.

"Franco, did you hear what I said in history class?"

"Yeah, who hasn't? It's all over the school." Franco looked down at the notebook and began scribbling his name.

"And you still want to sign it?" I was confused. Franco should be infuriated like all of my other friends, I thought.

"Yeah, I still want to sign it. If that's what you believe, that's up to you. I just want to wear my hat in school. See ya, Orville." Franco put his pen away and went through the swinging doors. I couldn't believe it. Franco was my friend. He

should've been bursting with anger, but he wasn't. Why didn't
he shake me and say, "What's wrong with you, Orville?" I just
didn't get it. The bell rang as my eyes wandered over to Gina.
I knew she had witnessed Franco signing the petition. Our
eyes met for a second because that's all my eyes could handle.
In that second, Gina's eyes asked, "Why, Orville?" I knew I
couldn't answer that question in public, but I had to answer
it for her. Case or no case, my friendship with Gina was too
sacred. I had hurt her, and I couldn't live with that. I decided
I'd call her after Driver's Ed. and tell her everything. She would
be angry but she would understand my motives. The one thing
I wouldn't be able to explain to her, because I couldn't explain it to myself, dealt with her ex—Franco. If he knew I
made anti-Semitic remarks, why did he still sign the petition?
He always stood up for what he believed in. This was not like
him. "Or maybe it is, and I never knew." I gulped and prayed
that I was wrong.

"So, Dan is sick?" Miss Turner's violet eyes questioned.

"Sick as a dog. He was going to go home right after lunch,"
I lied. I knew Franco had stayed at school the entire day.

"Something must be going around because Matt Dunn
stayed home sick, too." She threw me the keys.

"Considering his health problems, I'm not surprised." I
said.

"Yes, I feel sorry for Matt. His parents divorced when he
was just a little kid and his mother has to work two jobs to
pay off those medical bills."

"How did you know that?" I asked.

"He told me."

"Gee, that's funny. That kid never talks."

"It's amazing what people will tell you in the confines of a Driver's Ed. car. You would be surprised what I know about students in this school. Now, you better get behind the wheel." Miss Turner gave me a teasing smile, and I realized that the wildfire over my remarks couldn't have made its way into the teacher's room, because she was her usual playful self. I jumped into the driver's seat, switched on the ignition and asked, "What *do* people tell you?"

Miss Turner laughed for a second. "Well, let's see. We talk about everything, like music, movies, cars, and sports. Or where someone is going on a vacation. Like you, Orville. Is your family going to go visit your dad over in Ireland?"

"Who told you he was over there? I guess I must have."

"I told you that people talk. For example, have you thought of the gift you're going to get Vanessa Hyde for her surprise birthday party?"

"How did...?" I could feel my face turning red.

"People talk. And now you're blushing. That's OK. I won't tell anyone."

"People know about Vanessa and me, but ... it's just that we're ... ah, not, ah..."

"A couple yet," Miss Turner filled in the sentence.

"Right," I confessed.

"So, that means this birthday party will be a great opportunity to show her how much you care about her. So, what are you going to get her?" She was excited.

"I really don't know, Miss Turner. What do you think?" I

couldn't believe that I was asking advice about my love life from my Driver's Ed. teacher.

"Orville, I think it should be something really special and it can't be tacky. Wait … I know just the place to go for a gift. Head for Main Street."

"You mean, now?" I asked.

"Why not? We have plenty of time today considering the other two aren't here."

"All right." I shrugged and put my foot on the gas. I felt a little guilty that my mind was suddenly thinking about Vanessa and not the case. But, then I thought, it wouldn't be long until the rumor about me spread to Vanessa's school—Belltown Academy. I knew after Driver's Ed., in addition to Gina, I would have to call Vanessa and tell her the truth. If I didn't, there might not be any birthday party, or worse—any future for us. I didn't want to take that chance. I would do that later, but for now I was going to enjoy the few moments of just being a normal teenager—or at least I was going to try.

D'Leeder Family Jewelry Store had been a fixture in Belltown for over forty years, and this was the first time I had set foot in it. There was a logical reason why I hadn't been in before. It was decorated for royalty—oil paintings from Italy, Medieval tapestries, Oriental rugs, and Victorian love seats. Not to mention the jewelry! There was every style of jewelry one could imagine. This store was definitely for major leaguers. Unfortunately, my budget for Vanessa's gift didn't even qualify me as a minor leaguer. I was more like a little leaguer!

"Miss Turner, what are you, crazy? I can't afford anything in here," I said as I looked around, feeling as if I were trespassing.

"Maybe, and maybe not. I'm good friends with the owner," she said to me and then tapped her red index nail on a counter bell. "Grant, are you here?"

A second later, a man in his mid-forties came out. He had black hair, blue eyes, and a toothy smile. "Eleanor, is that you, my ..." he stopped talking when he saw me. "It is you and you brought a friend."

"Your name is Eleanor?" I exclaimed.

"Yes, Orville, it's no secret. Look in your yearbook."

"I know... it's just that..."

"It's pretty strange when you hear your teacher called by her first name, huh?" The man said what was on my mind.

"Exactly," I smiled as he put out his hand. "Orville Jacques."

"Orville, good to meet you. I'm Grant D'Leeder and this is my store. Actually, it was my father's and now I'm running it. So what can I do for you, Eleanor?"

"I'm really here for Orville. He has a birthday party to go to, and he wants to buy a special gift for that special girl." Miss Turner was enjoying this, and I was beginning to regret including her.

Grant chuckled. "So, the special girl, huh?"

"Well, I don't know about that. Anyway, I told Miss Turner that your store is way out of my price range."

"Yeah, you're probably right," he agreed.

Miss Turner gave him a look. "Grant, can I talk to you alone?"

"Oh … ah… sure."

She then turned to me. "Orville, why don't you go take a look at those paintings over there. I'll just be a second."

I nodded and went over to the paintings. As they whispered back and forth, I felt kind of stupid. After all, it was rather ridiculous that my Driver's Ed. teacher was doing my negotiating. Finally, Grant cracked up laughing, saying to her, "Really? That's a good one."

They seemed close and at the moment, I wondered if they were a couple. But, then I thought that was even more ridiculous, because he was almost twice her age. They were probably good friends, and he was just laughing at my embarrassment.

"OK, Orville. Miss Turner told me all about you and you remind me of this guy I once knew."

"Who?"

"Me," his smile broadened. "Now, does this girl have short or long hair?"

"Long, blonde hair. Why?" I asked as he was interrupted by the ringing phone.

He pointed at me. "Wonderful. You come by tomorrow, and I will have the perfect gift for you to look at. It would be fitting for you to have it." Grant smiled and picked up the phone. I wanted to think what this perfect gift would be, but it was time to stop daydreaming, because my next stop was home, where reality was waiting to greet me.

CHAPTER
FOUR

WHEN I GOT home there was a business card wedged into the door the The Shack. I pulled it out and studied its bold print: Detective Frank O'Halloran, Silver Shore Police Station (508) 555-1118. Underneath the print there was a handwritten message: "Please call me—S. O'Connell said you'd know why."

"The Harrison murder case," I said to myself. I put the card into my jean's pocket and opened my door. Of course, I would call Detective O'Halloran and answer his questions, but right now he was the last of my priorities. Gina was first, followed closely by Vanessa. I threw my backpack on my desk and headed for the phone. I was about to call Gina when I noticed the red, blinking light on my answering machine. Any other day, I would've been psyched to get messages, because the red, blinking light meant I had a life. But I had a feeling that these weren't social calls. I pressed the knob and it beeped, followed by: "Grow up, you Nazi pig." Click. Beep. "People like you make me sick." Click. Beep. "Pick up your history book, you idiot." Click. Beep. "Jacques, you should be that dumb guy they always have on the talk shows." Click. Beep. "Ignorant people like you is why this world is so messed up." Click. Beep. Click. Beep. Click. What did I get myself into? I wondered. I was feeling a little dizzy with regret. Was I over my head with this one? Could I live with the idea that kids in my school thought that I was a bigot? I had to remember it was for the greater good. Whoever was committing these hate crimes would now approach me to join them. But what if they didn't? What if he or she or they would rather not include anybody else in their hate campaign? Or worse, what if they were just passing through Belltown and the crimes stopped? Word would eventually get out that these crimes had occurred and people would whisper that it was Sue Edward or me. They wouldn't whisper about Paul Miller because he backed right off when he was confronted by his classmates. It was for that very reason Miller was still a suspect— whoever was defacing these homes didn't want to get caught so, of course, they wouldn't show their real feelings in public. Cowards commit crimes like these, and the way Paul Miller folded up like a tent showed me that he was still my number one coward.

The ringing phone shook me out of my state. I picked it up and harshly barked, "Yeah, what!"

"Orville, is that you?" the familiar voice on the other end asked.

I softened immediately. "Oh, sorry. I thought it was someone else. How are you doing Vanessa?"

"I'm fine. It's you I'm worried about. I talked to Christa Soderstrom and she told me all that stuff you said in history class. I told her I didn't believe it. It had to be a mistake. But then I saw Scotty Donovan and he said it's true. He had heard it too. Well, did you say that garbage about yarmulkes and Jewish people having special rights?"

"Yeah . . . Yeah, I said that stuff."

"You did?" She paused, then said, "I haven't known you a long time, but I know you have a beautiful heart. You would never feel that one group of people is better than another. You wouldn't. I just know you wouldn't. You care about people, and that's one of the reasons why I . . . Well . . . I just know there must be something more to this. What is it? Tell me the truth. What is going on?" she asked, even-toned.

I started to speak, and then a jolt of a memory struck me. It was Shane telling me not to tell anyone about the case for fear that he would get into trouble with the chief. If I told Vanessa, which had been my plan, she might try to defend me around her friends and it could slip out.

I took a deep breath. "Vanessa, what would you say if I told you I had a very good reason, but I can't tell you."

Her voice sounded angry. "I would say I'm about to hang . . ." and then she stopped. "Wait, wait. Wait just one second, Orville Jacques."

"What?" I asked.

"You forgot that I was once a client of yours. And I told you not to tell anyone about my case. I bet you're working on another case. Yeah, that's it. But, what would that have to do with saying all that stuff?"

"Vanessa, just trust me." I smiled. Somehow, she figured it out.

"One other thing. If you see me around town, pretend you hate me," I warned so I wouldn't lose my cover.

Vanessa laughed. "That won't be hard, 'cause you still didn't tell me what this case is about. You gotta tell me."

The phone beeped—call waiting to the rescue.

"Vanessa, that's my call waiting. This could be pretty important." I thought it may have been Gina, considering she had some time to think everything over.

"OK, Orville. I'll let you off the hook for now. Later."

No matter what everyone had told her, Vanessa believed in me. That was one of the main reasons why my feelings for her were growing.

I clicked over to the other line in a much better mood. "Hello?"

"Orville, it's Rabbi Spielman."

"Oh, hi, Rabbi. I suppose you want an update. Today I tried to establish a cover by ... "

"Orville, you can tell me that later. If I picked you up in five minutes, would you be ready to go?"

"Sure. Why?"

"They struck again last night."

Click.

The human side of me felt outraged that it had happened again, but the detective side knew that if they kept committing these heinous crimes, the chances were greater that they would eventually slip up and leave a clue. I was praying that *eventually* was *now*, as Rabbi Spielman's car pulled into my driveway.

On the ride over to the crime scene, I filled the Rabbi in on how I established my cover. He thought it was a great idea, except for the fact that I had put my reputation on the line. He began to second-guess himself for involving me, so I played it down, telling him that not many people reacted to my comments. I had a feeling if I told him about Gina's anger and the harassing phone calls I received, he would think I was risking too much and force me to end my investigation. Then, I'd have to reel the line in before the fish could even get a chance to nibble on the bait. I was the bait. I just needed more time to dangle from the hook, so I turned the conversation back onto the latest victims.

"What's the family's name?"

"Judy and Jonah Stein. They're good people, but they've had some personal troubles, and they have been thinking of moving out of Belltown for a while. I just hope this isn't the straw that breaks the camel's back." Rabbi Spielman took a left down a side street and then turned into the driveway in front of a rustic farmhouse.

"This is it. Here," he handed me a camera. "I told them that you were a student photographer documenting hate crimes."

I got out of the car. "That's pretty good, Rabbi. It sounds like something I'd make up."

I looked around for vandalism, but the house seemed to be in good shape.

"Where is all the destruction? The house looks OK to me."

"The house was untouched. The barn is another matter. It's out back. Follow me."

I walked behind Rabbi Spielman, following him down a narrow path for about fifty yards until he stopped in his tracks.

"There's your destruction." He motioned to the barn in front of us. I expected to see a run-down shed, but the barn was restored and it looked like an architect's dream, except for one thing: the new paint job and the shattered glass windows. I gasped. "How could someone do that?"

"They don't know any better." Rabbi Spielman shook his head and we were both silent for a minute while staring at the maroon spray-painted messages all over the front: "Go Home Jews," "Nazi's Rule," "Next stop Auschwitz."

Finally I was able to say, "Auschwitz. Wasn't that a concentration camp?"

"Yes, one of the worst. Hundreds of thousands of Jews were put to death there. Interesting that our friend couldn't spell Hitler, but managed Auschwitz. Perhaps there is more than one at work here, eh?"

"Whoever did this is an animal." I decided to put the camera to work and snapped some shots.

"An animal strikes out of fear. Whoever did this wanted to strike fear," a man's voice said behind us. "And they won!"

"Orville, this is Jonah Stein," Rabbi Spielman said.

"I am so sorry, Mr. Stein."

He shook my hand and tried to force a thank-you smile, but there was no way he could lose the grim expression on his face.

"Jonah, I know you are angry that I wanted to hush this up with the police, but …"

"Angry? I'm beyond angry, Rabbi. There should be newspaper reporters and television crews documenting this destruction, not covering it up. People should know that this still goes on! This is an assault on who we are! By covering it up you're not ..."

"Jonah, stop!" a woman yelled. I could tell she had been crying, and I guessed it was Mrs. Stein. "Jonah, the Rabbi already told you why. It could be a child or a group of children. If he can catch them and educate them, they won't have stained their lives for good." She wiped her eyes.

"And Judy, what about our lives? We're supposed to go on the Rabbi's hunch it's a kid because the first time they did it they spelled Hitler wrong? People who do this are all ages, and I wouldn't be surprised if they can't spell. This isn't just about some misguided kid." Jonah was furious and I didn't blame him.

"You're right, Jonah," Rabbi Spielman said. "It's also about the reputation of this town. The town was there for you at the toughest time in your life. Now, I'm asking you to be there for them." Rabbi Spielman looked at him while I wondered what that tough time had been. The Rabbi then moved closer. "Jonah, it is hard. I know it is. But, this wonderful community that was there for you could be ruined if this gets out."

Rabbi Spielman then took Jonah's arms in his hands. "Jonah, don't get me wrong. I have put my own timetable on this. If the police and the person I have hired to investigate can't find the guilty party in a week, I promise you, I will go public. That is one of the reasons I brought Orville here, to take pictures of the destruction."

Jonah calmed down. "I do owe this town. I guess a few more days wouldn't hurt. Now, Orville, I hope you have a lot of film, because inside it's ten times worse."

I just nodded. I was speechless, reflecting on what I had just witnessed. Rabbi Spielman was taking a tremendous risk, but he was thinking of the greater good—a town's good reputation, and perhaps some misguided young person. The doubt I had earlier about taking the case vanished. I was embarrassed that I even had doubt as I followed Mr. Stein into the barn while stepping around pieces of broken glass.

When I entered the barn, the setting triggered a memory of a childhood toy I once had—a kaleidoscope. I used to spend hours looking through the kaleidoscope adjusting the dial, creating various colored designs. The design I was looking at now was hundreds of shattered pieces of multi-colored glass strewn across the floor and workbench. Unlike my designs, this one wasn't created by the hand of a child; it was constructed by the hand of hate. I was about to ask Mr. Stein why he had so much colored glass when he clued me in.

"This is my workshop—or I should say, this *was* my workshop. My hobby is working with stained glass. I had probably close to a hundred pieces finished. I was even thinking of selling them to some of the tourist stores on the Cape. But now …" He grabbed a broom and began sweeping the glass into a pile. I wanted to say how sorry I was, but I knew those words would be no source of comfort for him, so I decided to try to keep it low-key. "So, do you make stained glass windows?" I said as I snapped a shot of spray-painted swastika above his workbench.

"I've done a couple of windows in my house, but I mostly do window and wall ornaments. I even make my own frames for them. One of the reasons we've stayed here is the inspiration I get from the Cape landscape." For a moment he had forgotten what had happened, so I thought I should keep asking him questions.

"How does the Cape landscape inspire you?"

"Well, I'll take a walk or a bike ride and I'll see something like a lobster trap washed up on a beach, or a fishing boat with the pink sunset in the background, and then I'll come home and create that same scene with my glass." He stopped and looked back down at the pile of colors he had swept into his dustpan. "But, I suppose I could find inspiration somewhere else." He dumped the smashed pile into a garbage can.

"So, you're going to move just because of this?"

"No. I have other reasons."

I was about to ask him what they were when I spotted a picture frame that had fallen under the workbench. I picked it up and in the frame there was a picture of a boy my age. He looked just like Mr. Stein.

"Is this your son?" I asked.

"Yes," was all he said and went back to sweeping.

"He looks my age, but I don't think I know him. Does he go to Belltown High?"

"He did for a little while. That picture was taken a few years back."

"That explains it. Is he in college?"

Mr. Stein looked up. "No. My boy is dead."

I almost dropped the picture out of shock. I took another look at the photo. The boy's eyes and smile seemed so alive.

"I'm sorry, Orville. I shouldn't have sprung that on you like that. It's just so hard for me to say it unless I'm asked."

"I understand, Mr. Stein. He looked just like you. What was his name?"

"Michael." He put the broom down and took the picture from me and stared at it. "He was the best. He ... ah ... was riding his bike one day and a man ... ran a stop sign. If he had just stopped. If he just stopped for even a few seconds, my boy would be alive."

The pain in his voice ripped at my heart, and I felt my eyes watering.

"That's the other reason I want to leave Belltown. Too many bad memories. My wife is expecting, and she wants to stay. She says Michael would want it that way. And she's right. He loved this town. But, how are we going to try and raise another child when we are faced with this?" He pointed at the swastika and then headed outside to join his wife and Rabbi Spielman. I wanted to tell Mr. Stein that he shouldn't give up because of a few bad people, but that would be easy for me, considering I was not in his shoes. I wiped my eyes and continued to take pictures.

After about ten minutes, the Steins and Rabbi Spielman came into the barn.

"Orville, why don't you come into the house and have something to eat?" Mrs. Stein asked.

"Thanks, but I'm not really hungry." The scene had made me lose my appetite. I moved across the room to snap another photo when Mr. Stein said, "Watch out. They knocked over some house paint while they went out the back window. It's still sticky."

I looked down and saw a drying puddle of white paint.

"Why did they go out the back?"

"They must've heard us coming. You see, we figure this must've happened when we were at the movies. We went to the late show, but it was terrible, so we left early," Mrs. Stein said, as my eyes searched the floor of the barn. And then I saw it.

"Come over here! Take a look!" I pointed to the floor.

"What is it?" Rabbi Spielman asked.

"Exactly what I was praying for," I said, as I focused and snapped photos of my first clue—a white print of a heel. I didn't know if it was the heel of a shoe or a boot. Or if it was made by a man or woman or boy or girl. But, what I did know was whoever was running around Belltown committing these crimes was running around in the proof I needed to put them away.

After the fifth time Gina hung up on me before I could even get a word out, I decided to give up calling her. I would have to tell her about everything face to face, but the problem was catching her when nobody else was around so I wouldn't blow my cover. The next phone call I made was to Detective Frank O'Halloran of the Silver Shore Police Department. He was a by-the-book officer who asked me the standard questions that I had no problem answering. But when it came time for *my* questions like, "Who found Clark Harrison's body?" or "Do they have any suspects?" Detective Frank O'Halloran thanked me for my time and hung up. Fortunately, there was another detective whose last name also began with an O who had always filled me in—Shane O'Connell.

"Orville, you really shouldn't be thinking of the Harrison murder case. It's out of my jurisdiction and it's *way* out of yours. You should be thinking of the case I let you in on. Did Rabbi Spielman bring you to the Steins' barn?"

"Yeah, that's the main reason for calling you. Someone left a heel print in some white paint. I don't know if it was from a shoe or a boot."

"It came from a boot. A male's boot, to be more precise. The company that makes that style of boot is Cape Adventurer."

"How did you find all that out?"

"Remember, we're both working on this case. Officer Jameson found the print and it looked familiar. We just compared it to the Cape Adventurer boots I have in my closet— same style print. But I am happy to hear that you spotted that print." Shane sounded like a proud father and when it came to my investigating, he was. I think deep down he felt I was a lot like him when he was my age, and that's why he enjoyed teaching me.

"Almost everybody on the Cape wears Cape Adventurer boots in the winter. Even me. So that's going to be hard to track down," I said.

"Nice pun, Orville." Shane laughed.

"What?" I didn't get it.

"Seriously, Orville, this is where your services could be

extremely valuable for this investigation. I can't risk having any of my men go to your school tomorrow to look at everyone's footwear."

"Why? I mean if they find the white heel they'll find their guy."

"Yes, but if there is more than one person involved, word will get out. If that person is just passing through town, he'll be long gone before we can question him. So, you keep your eyes glued to the ground tomorrow and then call me. I should be back in Belltown by then. But if I'm not, hold your tongue till you get me. I don't want anybody to know that you're involved in this."

"I understand, but where are you going?"

"I have to go to Boston on some personal business. In fact, I wanted to be on the road before seven so I gotta burn."

"OK, but before you go, Shane. Did Detective O'Halloran say anything about the Harrison murder case? Like who found the body? Suspects? Stuff like that?"

Shane gave a defeated laugh. "Harrison's body was found in his doorway at six in the morning. Who do you think found it?" He quizzed me. It was a game we always played.

I thought for a minute. Who would be up at that hour?

"I got it. The paper boy."

"As always, Orville, I'm impressed. The paperboy didn't have much info except that he had seen a blue pickup truck leave the neighborhood a few minutes earlier. But, I don't have to tell you, a blue pickup truck on the Cape is as common as fish in the ocean. Frankie's got his work cut out for him. Well, I'll talk to you later. Bye."

"Yeah, later." I hung up and stretched out in my chair.

Why does Shane go to Boston so much? I wondered, and stared down at my own Cape Adventurer boots for a minute. Then, something caught the corner of my eye, and I glanced over at my door. I hopped out of my chair and grabbed the envelope. It was a red envelope with black ink and block lettering on the front—Orville Jacques. I jerked my door open and looked outside, and when I was satisfied that no one was there, I shut the door and ripped open the envelope. I felt my eyes widening as I read. I just couldn't believe what I was reading. My plan had really worked. I had dangled from the hook and the fish had just taken the bait!

CHAPTER
FIVE

AFTER I READ the letter, my eyes raced back to the top of the paper. I had to read it again to make sure I wasn't dreaming.

Dear Orville Jacques,
Do you ever feel that people do not understand you? That they don't share your beliefs? We think you probably felt that way today in your history class. No one there to support you. ALONE. But, Orville, you are not alone. You have many friends who feel the same way you do. There is a brotherhood waiting with open arms. We are waiting for you. Come join us. Go to Old Winslow's Bait Shop at 11:30 tonight. Cut eyeholes in a white sheet and bring that and a green apple with you. Come alone and then you won't be.
A Friend

My digital clock flicked 6:56. I called Shane but he had already left for Boston. It was probably for the best anyway. I figured whoever they were they would be watching me to see if I was legit. I had no choice but to go solo and try and gain their trust. I had plenty of time to get ready. All I needed to stash in my backpack was the white sheet with the eyeholes. I wasn't surprised by the sheet. Whoever these people were, they probably practiced their hate like the Ku Klux Klan. What did surprise me was the green apple. What did that have to do with anything? I knew I would have to wait a little longer for that question to be answered. Fortunately, my mom loved green apples more than anything in the world, so there were plenty to choose from in the fruit basket. There was one other thing I packed in my inside coat pocket—a mini spy camera Shane had given me for Christmas. The chances of using it were slim, but I figured I'd rather be safe than sorry. Now all I had to do was wait. Of all the instructions, waiting was the hardest part.

By 11:00 Mom was always asleep, but I figured I'd better double check to be safe. I pushed the drapes aside out of The Shack window. The house was in darkness. "Perfect. Thanks for The Shack, Mom and Dad," I said to myself. I would have been out of the investigating business if they hadn't winterized our garage and transformed it into my own place. It was extremely easy to sneak out of The Shack, but I made it a point never to do that unless I was sneaking out for a case.

I didn't want to abuse the freedom they had given me. Of course, I knew if they ever caught me, they wouldn't have quite the same view I had on the subject, so I was always careful. But on this night, I had to be extra careful, considering Mom confessed that ever since Dad went to Ireland, she had become a light sleeper. With that in mind, I slipped out my door and crept through my backyard and then eased over the fence.

Ironically, I knew it would be safer to cut through the backyards of my neighborhood instead of using the sidewalk and risk exposure from the streetlights. When I felt I was a safe distance from my house, I moved onto the street. Old Winslow's Bait Shop was located directly across from Belltown Harbor, which was about a twenty-five minute walk. Fortunately, the snow that had paralyzed Belltown the previous week had all but melted and the night was uncharacteristically balmy. That didn't mean I was warm, though! I had a nervous chill flowing through my body as I walked along, wondering what was waiting for me at Old Winslow's Bait Shop. I knew it couldn't be Old "Chet" Winslow himself because he always closed shop in the winter and headed to Florida. Maybe that's why they—it did say "they" in the letter—were meeting there. They knew Old Winslow was away. I continued on for the next twenty minutes while thinking of how I was going to act when I met them. I decided I'd act like an angry young man who was thankful that there were people who understood him.

"Another five minutes," I whispered to myself.

And then what? I wondered.

I directed my flashlight at the sign hanging at the front door of Old Winslow's Bait Shop. It read: "Closed for Season. See ya in May." I jiggled the doorknob but the door was locked. I held my flashlight low to the ground as I moved cautiously to the back door of the shop. I jiggled again—locked. I checked my watch—11:32. Was this a trick? I wondered, as I flashed my light quickly to see if anyone was following me. There was no sign of anyone. Maybe it was a prank, I thought, as I looked around. The full moon gave a soft light on the harbor. My eyes searched while my ears listened to the eerie stillness of the night. There were hardly any sounds at all except the docked fishing boats. They creaked as the gentle silver surf moved from side to side. The other sound was the swinging bell buoy that I knew all too well; it rang every few seconds. A strong quiver suddenly shocked my body. Something told me to flash my light to the right. The light speared the dark and a loud bang followed—it was a ladder slamming to the ground. At first I jumped back out of fright, but then I ran over to the ladder and whipped my light out in front of me— a figure was running full-speed down the road, but was too far away to identify. Then it came together in my head. The person had been coming down the ladder when my flash-light surprised them. I flashed my light up to the top of Old Winslow's and spotted a blood-red balloon tied to the gutter of the shop. I turned off my light, put it into my pocket, picked up the ladder and placed it against the side of the bait shop. I climbed the ladder, which was about twelve feet, and then grabbed the balloon. Taped to the balloon was another letter. It read: "Go to the clearing in the woods behind Coolidge Cranberry Bogs. Go NOW."

I took a breath and shook my head. I untied the balloon and let the night sky take it. Part of me was beginning to think it was a prank and someone was playing with me. But the other part thought it could be the real thing. I had to listen to that part. If it were a prank, the worst thing I could lose was a few hours of sleep. Like I'd be able to sleep anyway! But, what I was about to find out was no joke …

I thought long and hard before deciding which route to take to the clearing behind Coolidge Cranberry Bogs. I knew if I took the direct route, which meant cutting through the bogs, it would take me only about ten minutes. Since I was sick of walking that was the easiest way to go. But, then I thought, whoever that full-sprint figure had been, he would be expecting me to come that way. If this was some sort of trap, I didn't want to just walk right into it. I had to have the element of surprise on my side. Even though it would be another twenty-five minute walk, I chose to circle the cranberry bogs and go through the woods, which were on the other side of the clearing.

The winter sun hadn't been able to penetrate the huge trees, which was fortunate for me because there was still snow in the woods. Therefore, I didn't have to risk using my flashlight for lighting. The full moon was my guide as it bounced off the snow, giving me just enough of a glow to follow. I lumbered along for a couple of minutes in silence, except for my footsteps and breathing. Out of nowhere came a cracking noise. I went a couple of more steps—crack. I placed the location of the sound and almost laughed. I had been the cause of the cracking. My boots had been snapping a half-buried briar patch, and the thorns were tearing my lower pant leg. I shook my leg for a few seconds, and I finally broke free from the thorns.

"Oh, no," I whispered, as I realized that the half-buried patch below my legs was nothing compared to the menacing wall of thorns that waited up ahead. There was no way around the patch. "How am I going to get over that?"

I didn't like the idea of backtracking and going another twenty-five minutes. I had to think of a plan. A memory then zapped my brain—a bunch of friends and I played a nerf football game in the clearing a few years before. We had the same problem. How did we get past the briar patch? I wondered. "That's right," I said as I spotted a small opening. I remembered that if you went through the opening, a path widened that zigzagged through the thorns. I tucked my body into the opening and slowly moved along the path, knowing one wrong move and the hanging razor-sharp thorns would let me know. Thankfully, I was careful enough to dodge every one of them. When I made it through, I let out a sigh of relief. There was an old dirt road that ran parallel to the patch. I remembered that the road lead to another group of trees and beyond that was the clearing. I hunched down, knowing I didn't have much farther to go. As I moved along the road, my ears strained. There was a faint sound of distant voices. My adrenaline began to pump again because the closer I got, the louder the voices became. Also, the snow-glow light became even brighter as I approached the trees before the clearing until I was there. I stood in absolute shock for a second. I just couldn't believe what I saw. Then my common sense woke up, and I lunged to the ground and crawled behind a tree for safety. I sat up huffing and puffing and pressed my back against the tree. My adrenaline was pumping now, but my nerves were weakening. I wanted to hide behind the tree forever, but the force that always controls me was telling me that I couldn't hide. Finally, I took a gasp of breath, turned around and moved my right eye around the tree. Was this Belltown? I still couldn't believe it, but there they were, right in front of me—a dozen people wearing white sheets and holding torches in front of a huge portrait of Adolf Hitler!

"We are Hitler's sons!" they chanted at the portrait, while waving their torches in unison.

Now what? I wondered. Do I go out there and ask to join their group? I thought for a moment and then my trembling fingers unzipped my backpack and pulled out my white sheet and green apple. I stuffed the green apple into my coat pocket.

"You're crazy," I scolded myself, as if I were talking to a stranger, and then put the sheet over my head. I was about to make my move to the clearing when I heard the revving of a car engine. No one uses this road anymore, I thought, but then headlights flashed through the trees. The car was coming down the dirt road and it was heading my way. I jumped across the road and slid face first behind a group of snow-covered bushes. I listened for the car and it sounded like it was parked only yards away. I couldn't hear anything except for my heavy panting that seemed even louder inside the sheet. After a few seconds, I heard the car door slam shut. I inched my head around the bushes and peeked through the narrow eyeholes. It was a man, but I couldn't make out his face because his back was to me. He slipped a scarlet-colored sheet over his head and then tied the rope-belt around his waist. I gasped lightly, but not light enough, because he jerked his body around and scanned the area. My eyeballs froze and my muscles tensed. I knew one slight move, and it could be the end for me. Finally, he gave a reluctant shrug and continued into the clearing. The dozen people roared at the Scarlet Man's arrival and waved their flames. The roaring was the perfect noise cover for me to run. I could have run the other way, but that uncontrollable force made me dive behind my original hiding place. I got settled and used my right eye again.

"Let the great one speak!" one of the hoods demanded, and everyone fell silent as the Scarlet Man went into the middle of the clearing. They encircled him as he raised his hands.

"As you know, I am here to lead all of you to a better life, because I have the power to talk to the greatest leader of all." He pointed over to the Hitler portrait. "He tells me … he tells me, Sons of Hitler, that this town is not taking us seriously. We have to make them listen. We have to make a statement soon. We have to let the people of Belltown know that the Sons of Hitler have come to Belltown and this time we have come to stay! We will rid it of the scum that exists, and replace it with our own people. The great white race!" They gave a thunder-

The Secrets of the Twisted Cross 65

ing cheer, but suddenly stopped when a member in a white sheet came running from the other side of the clearing.

"Where have you been?" the Scarlet Man demanded.

The member came closer and whispered into the Scarlet Man's ear.

"What? You fool!!" He pushed the member down to the ground. "I am the leader of the Sons of Hitler, not you! You have no right to recruit a member without my telling you!" Scarlet Man clenched his fist and the person put his hands up to deflect the punch. It didn't work. The Scarlet Man connected and hit him twice. The member lay on the ground moaning in pain. Scarlet Man yelled down at him, "I checked on this Orville Jacques. He's trouble! I don't care if he says he hates all Jews and blacks. He's lying! He's trying to get to us!"

My eyes almost popped out of my head at the sound of my name. He was onto me!

"He's probably at the police station now! You're so stupid! Can't you do anything right? This meeting is over! I will contact you all!" Scarlet Man began to storm from the clearing. At that moment, I remembered his car was only fifteen feet away. All I needed was his license plate number. I ran low to the ground over to the car and noticed it wasn't a car at all. It was a blue pickup truck. A blue pickup truck… Where did I hear about a blue pickup truck? Forget about that, get the plate number. I crouched down to read the number, but it was covered with mud. I wiped the globs of mud off the first number. It was a P, but as I was clearing the second letter I felt a strange gust of wind. Then I realized my white sheet had flown off my head. I turned around and saw Scarlet Man holding my sheet in his hands.

"It's you." He was in shock for a second, and it was just enough time for me to take the green apple out of my coat pocket and fire it at him. I don't know where I hit him, but I know I did, because he let out a grunt of pain. I bolted down the dirt road and only got about thirty yards when I heard, "He's here! He's here! Jacques is here! Get him!"

I looked to the clearing and saw the white sheets and torches scampering my way. I sprinted another fifty yards and then looked back. The torches had separated and they were coming in different directions. I stayed on the dirt road until I heard the truck's engine racing, and sensed the headlights catching my shadow. At that point, I swayed out of control back into the brush. The truck continued down the road, but the members with the torches were still out there. Their torches looked like fireflies on a summer's night buzzing from every direction. I was going in circles as I tried to avoid them, and I was beginning to feel like a spinning top. When I realized I had done a complete circle, I really felt dizzy. The briar patch was straight ahead. I looked back and saw six of the random torches come together as one. They were right behind me, and I had no choice but to try to maneuver through the wall of thorns again. But this time, I couldn't slow down as I wove wildly through the zigzag path. And this time, I wasn't as lucky as before. The piercing thorns dug their claws into my scalp, face, legs, and arms. I pulled my body through the torture and the pain was sapping my energy. I cursed as the blood flowed freely from my scalp, and I finally made it to the other side. My obvious agony didn't frighten my pursuers from following. I heard the same horrific yells. I looked back at the yells and saw only one of my pursuers was able to make it through the patch, because it was now going up in flames. Someone's torch must have ignited it, I thought, as I glanced at the fiery wall. The fire had helped my odds considerably. All I had to do was outrun the member behind me and I'd be home free. The problem was that my legs weren't listening to the fear screaming from my brain. He was gaining, fast. I knew I couldn't outrun him. There was no chance. I dove down in my tracks and he tumbled over me. I jumped on top of him, and began to punch him. But he was big, and it wouldn't be long before he got control. He was yelling something, but I wasn't listening to him. I was listening to my mind that was pleading with me to at least grab the sheet. I got a grasp of it and yanked it off as he yelled, "Orville! Stop!"

And I did stop. In fact, I froze. I couldn't move at all. It was surreal. The pain from the thorns was no match for the pain I had just uncovered. There, staring at me were eyes that I knew so well. But now I wasn't sure if I had ever known them at all. They were the eyes of one of my best friends, Dan "Franco" Francais. They were the eyes of a member of a hate group. A member of the Sons of Hitler . . .

"Did you get him?" the voices shouted from beyond the smoke and flames.

"Orville, get out of here," I think Franco whispered. But I still was in shock, staring at him in disbelief.

"Get out of here," he pushed at me. "They'll kill you if they catch you."

His warning finally penetrated my consciousness. I gave him one last look and shook my head in disgust before sprinting away. When I made it back to the main road along Cranberry Beach, the severe pain from my physical and mental injuries came together and stabbed my upper chest.

"Why Franco? Why Franco?" I asked over and over again as I walked in a daze while wiping my blurry eyes. It was like I was in a foggy maze, and I was unaware of my surroundings. I just kept walking in a trance, and that was probably the reason I wasn't able to hear the racing engine until it was almost too late. It was the blinding headlights that brought me back to the moment. I couldn't make out what was behind the headlights, but I didn't have to. I knew it was the blue pickup truck barreling down the road, headed directly for me.

"Oh no!" I yelled as I tried to run, but my body was sluggish and was giving up on me. It was overtime, and my body was stunned that it still had to perform. But this wasn't a basketball game. This was my life. I had to fight the urge to quit. The headlights were only a few feet away when my will to survive kicked in. I spotted the wood fence that enclosed the Cranberry Beach parking lot. I gave a running leap and dove over the fence. The screeching truck skidded to a stop just missing the fence. I lay stretched out on the ground until I heard the truck door slam shut, followed by rustling footsteps. Wobbling to my feet I almost lost my balance but was able to stumble forward and head for the camouflage of the dunes on the beach. The fear was back as I kicked through the sand and ducked in and out of the dunes. I looked back and despite his running in a sheet, I realized the Scarlet Man was gaining. I wouldn't be able to outrun him much longer. I had to outthink him if I had any chance for survival. I slid down the side of a dune to the beach and then looked up. I saw him on top of another dune, scanning the area, but he didn't see me. He thought I was still hiding in the dunes. I knew this would give me at least a couple of minutes to find another hiding place. But now I was on the open beach. There really was no place to hide, unless I jumped into the ocean. I knew in my weakened state, there was no way I could expose my body to the bone-chilling waters. Then I spotted a bulldozer near the end of the beach. The bulldozer was probably on the beach to deposit sand. Maybe if I hid in the cab of the bulldozer, I'd be safe, I thought. I had no other choice, because where the beach ended, the ocean began. I sprinted twenty yards and then tugged on the cab door of the bulldozer—it was locked. I looked around, frantically trying to figure out my next move. Then I noticed the massive scoop of the bulldozer in the moonlight. It was about seven feet off the ground. I clutched onto the side and shimmied along its arms until I got to the scoop. I looked in and there was a few feet of sand in it. I eased down into the scoop and waited. The question was, what was I waiting for? I prayed that I wasn't a sitting duck waiting for him to find me. I clung to the hope that he would keep searching the dunes, that he'd rationalize I'd be crazy to go into the open beach because there was no place to hide. I lay there and watched the stars in a sky that was getting lighter. The morning light was beginning to crack through. Just another fifteen minutes and it would be too light. He'd realize that it was too risky to keep searching for me. I just had to wait and watch the sky and pray. But the longer the stars began to fade, the longer my curiosity peaked. Finally, I sat up and peered over the scoop and shuddered—there he was, about sixty feet away, looking down at the sand at something. I gulped hard when I realized what it was—my backpack! I didn't even remember dropping it. I also thought that I had run close enough along the shoreline so the surf would erase my footprints. The way he looked down at the sand as he walked along told me that I was wrong. The trail was slowly leading him to the bulldozer. I ducked back down. Could I jump down and outrun him? What if he had a gun? There was no escape this time. I heard his heavy breathing above the tumbling waves. He was beside the bulldozer. He tugged on the door and grunted in anger. I was paralyzed with fright and all I could do was watch the sky and pray that the remaining stars would vanish into daylight. But the light sky that I thought was my savior actually showed me something else. On the top of the scoop there was blood—my blood. I had left a blood trail. I knew it wouldn't take long for him to follow that trail and see that the footprints and blood ended at the bulldozer. So, if I wasn't in the cab, there was only one other place to look—in the scoop. I could hear him huffing as he stood below. I crouched into a ball in a futile attempt to hide, but I knew I couldn't as his fingers grasped the top of the scoop and he was lifting himself up. His fingers were inches away as I studied the fire-red ruby ring on his finger. I clenched my fist and cocked my arm waiting for his masked face to appear above the shovel. But, as he was lifting his body, two seagulls swooped down and landed on the top of the scoop right next to his hands. They squawked at him and then pecked at his hands until he moaned in pain and let go of the scoop, falling to the sand. The distant wailing of a fire engine shrieked along the beach road. I heard the Scarlet Man say something under his breath. From the anger in his voice it sounded like he was cursing, but I wasn't sure because he was talking in a foreign tongue. A second later, I heard him run away. I peeked over the teeth of the scoop and the Scarlet Man was half way down the beach. A couple of minutes later, I heard his truck hauling down the road. I jumped from the scoop and tumbled onto the sand. I got up, brushed the sand off, and stared at the two seagulls squawking overhead.

I took a deep breath as I watched them fly out to sea heading toward the rising sun. Thanks to the gulls, I would live another day to see that sun set. At least, that is what I hoped as I jogged home.

CHAPTER
SIX

When I got back to The Shack the temptation to fall right into bed was overwhelming, but I knew sleep wasn't an option, because I only had a couple of hours to get ready for school. By the reflection staring back from the mirror, I needed every minute of that time to clean up. I had streaks of dried blood painted across my face, and a few thorns still stuck in my chin. I winced as I pulled them out, and then washed my wounds. When I was finished sticking on the Band-Aids, I took another look into the mirror and realized I resembled an Egyptian mummy. I knew I would have to leave early for school so Mom wouldn't see my disfigured face. I mean, what kind of excuse could I make up? I was attacked by a cat while I was asleep? No way. That wouldn't fly. But before I left for school, I wanted to write down every important detail of the night while it was still fresh in my head. I got out my detective journal and began scribbling:

1. Sons of Hitler—Was that the official name of the hate group? Or was he just saying that they were like sons of Hitler? I think since they were worshipping a portrait of Hitler, that it is the name of their group. Remember to ask Shane to look up "Sons of Hitler." They could be a national hate group organization.

2. Man in scarlet sheet, a.k.a. Scarlet Man—He was driving a blue pickup truck with a license plate that began with the letter P.

I stopped writing for a second and said, "Where did I hear about a blue pickup truck? Wait a minute ... I've got it! There was a blue pickup truck seen leaving the murder scene of antiques dealer, Clark Harrison's house. Could that be the same truck?" But then I thought of what Shane had said about blue pickup trucks on the Cape: "They're as common as fish in the ocean." It was probably just a coincidence. After all, what would Harrison and the metal trunk have to do with a hate group? I jotted it down anyway, just in case.

3. The Scarlet Man was wearing a fire-red ruby ring on his finger. Whoever is wearing that ring is our man!!

4. Franco—How could he be involv ...

I couldn't finish as I threw down my pen and said, "It just doesn't make sense. He can't be a racist."

"I hope you're talking about me." The voice behind me made me jump and take a defensive stance.

Franco put his hands up. "Orville, calm down. It's me."

"And that's supposed to make me calm? You ... you ... you ..." I was boiling so much I couldn't speak.

"Orville, I just heard you say, 'It doesn't make sense. He can't be a racist.' And you're right. I mean, how long have you known me?"

"Since first grade, but it doesn't matter. I guess I never knew you at all." I glared at him.

"You're some great detective, Jacques." Franco shot back.

"What do you mean?" His anger bewildered me.

"Did you ever think why I was running around with those fools in the middle of the night?"

"Stop the riddles. Get to the point."

"The point? The point, my friend, is only a few days ago I helped you chase Ivan Petralkov out of our town. Who knows how many lives we saved. It is a bond that Gina, you, and I will always have because other than Detective O'Connell and the CIA, no one knows about it. So, do you think a few days later I'm going to join a bunch of spineless wimps who get their kicks chanting 'We are Hitler's sons?' C'mon, Orville, think!"

"I am thinking. I'm thinking you dumped Gina because she is Jewish. You signed my petition even though I said some anti-Semitic stuff in class and you were at the meeting wearing a white sheet. Tell me, Dan, what's there to think about?"

"Orville, I could say the same things about you, but I had the sense to figure it out when all the members of Sons of Hitler were chasing you. You had said all that stuff to try to infiltrate the group, just like I did."

"You?" I asked, maybe the puzzle was finally coming together.

"Yeah, Orville, thanks to you, and the Ivan case, I caught the detective bug. So, when I accidentally found out about the Sons of Hitler I saw my opportunity to do some undercover work. I think they were really beginning to trust me, too. That is, until you messed everything up back there. One of the members somehow was able to see through the fire. He saw me let you go. I had to fight my way out of there." Franco pointed to his eye and I noticed for the first time that it was a mixed shade of purple and blue.

"Awww, man. How could I be so stupid? Franco, man, awww man, Franco, I'm sorry I thought that." I felt terrible.

Franco broke into a smile. "Orville, it's OK. I did the same thing with you. Everyone at school was talking about what you said and part of me was like, 'that's not Orville. It can't be. He must've found out about the group.' But, then there was that question, maybe I never really knew Orville Jacques. Now I realize how stupid I was, too."

I smiled and held my hand out. "No hard feelings. Friends?" He grinned and his hand locked with mine. "Friends . . . and partners?"

My smile broadened. "Yeah, partners."

Despite my fatigue and lingering pain, for the next ten minutes, while I listened to how Franco was recruited into the group, I felt like a million dollars. Everything about his actions now made sense, and the tremendous burden had been lifted. I didn't say a word as he recounted how he accidentally uncovered the group.

"I had just had gym class. We played floor hockey, and I stayed to help Mr. Curran collect all the sticks and put the nets away. So, when I went into the locker room to change into my regular clothes, I was all alone. I went over to my locker, and I noticed the locker next to mine was slightly open. Well, last year I forgot to lock mine and someone snagged my sneakers. So, I figured I'd be a good guy and lock it. But when I looked for the lock, I realized it didn't have one. It was one of the unissued lockers because it was empty except for one thing. There was a letter taped inside on the back of the locker. It said something like: 'Sons of Hitler—Tonight's Meeting—Same Place, Same Time.' Well, when I saw the name Hitler I said to myself, 'Oh man, we have a hate group in our own school.' Orville, I love this school and I love this town. I knew this was my chance to go undercover, but I knew I'd have to break things off with Gina. She would have to hate me if I wanted my cover to work," Franco stopped and shook his head. "I probably should've told her anyway. It was cruel and stupid. She's never going to forgive me."

"You're not the only one she's mad at. It was pretty stupid of both of us. But, Franco, I don't understand why you didn't tell me?"

"At first I didn't think anyone would believe you to be a racist if you went undercover with me. So, I figured I should go solo and not tell anyone until I had the goods. Which I still don't have. And then, when you said that stuff, I thought, Wow, good thing I didn't include him. I never knew he was like that."

"OK, that makes sense, and you were right because the leader was right onto me."

"I know. I almost died when he was shouting all that stuff about you. And then when he yelled, 'He's here. Jacques is here.' Man, I didn't know what to do." Franco was getting upset rehashing the scene and I felt even guiltier.

"How did you get the Sons of Hitler to include you?"

"I wrote them a stupid letter saying that I was going out with a Jewish girl, but just found out all this stuff about Jews from my Dad. It went on to say that I dumped the girl because I should be with my own. It went on and on with this terrible made-up stuff. I mean, I'm a quarter Jewish myself, but those idiots bought it. They slipped a letter into my locker inviting me to a meeting. I had to bring a white sheet and a bag of jelly beans, of all things." Franco shrugged his shoulders.

"They told me to bring a green apple. I don't even like green apples," I said.

"Well, I hate jelly beans, but fortunately my mom loves them. Jelly beans are her favorite."

"Wait! That's strange, because green apples are one of my mom's favorite things in the world."

We were both quiet for a minute.

Franco snapped his fingers. "I got it. I went to one meeting before this one. In that meeting, they didn't let me put on my sheet until I gave the leader the bag of jelly beans. He said something like, 'New member, we know what you look like and we know what you love.' I wanted to tell him that I hated jelly beans but I kept quiet, but now I get it. I love my mother."

"Yeah?" I didn't get it.

"The members knew my mom loved jelly beans. That was his way of telling me that my family was being watched. So, if you leave the group . . ."

"There could be trouble for you and your family." I grimly filled in the sentence.

"Or, there *will* be trouble." Franco nodded.

Walking into school I noticed that kids were still whispering and pointing behind my back. Of course, the bandages on my face didn't exactly help me blend into the crowd. Paul Miller walked with Craig Hampton behind me and coughed sarcastically under his breath, "Nice face." Hampton laughed and slapped Miller on the back.

I turned around and spit my own sarcasm, "Gee, Miller. That's hilarious. Boy, Jay Leno has nothing on you."

"Shut up, Jacques." Miller moved into my face and I glanced down at his feet—he was wearing sneakers. I moved my eyes over to Craig Hampton's feet—sneakers. I would have sworn that Miller would have been the person wearing the Cape Adventurer boot with the painted white heel. I banged a locker beside me in frustration. Miller and Hampton snickered, thinking that my obvious agitation was caused from Miller getting into my face.

"That's right, Jacques. Hit the locker, because you know if you hit me, you'd go down and you wouldn't get up."

I chuckled back, "Miller, you've seen too many westerns. Get outta my way."

"And if I don't?" He moved closer, and normally I probably would have been nervous, but considering what I had just been through, I thought the scene was amusing, especially the old "And if I don't" line. So, I laughed even more and turned the question back on him. "I don't know, Miller. What happens if you don't get out of my way?"

This seemed to puzzle Miller and Hampton, because they looked at each other and then Miller said, "Craig, let's go. I gotta get to class. Hey, Jacques. Don't forget. I'm watching you."

I laughed again. "Of course you are, Miller."

Every tough-guy line Miller always said seemed to be stolen from all the bad TV teen dramas.

I had to turn my attention back to my job, which was looking at small groups of people chatting at their lockers and check their footwear. Each time I spotted someone wearing Cape Adventurer boots, I moved closer to look for any signs of white paint on the heel. Not once did I see any. I hoped the guilty party hadn't used paint thinner. That was a possibility. Or maybe they just didn't wear the boots to school. I had to keep looking and not get discouraged, because the school day had just begun, and there were a lot of feet in my school. The good thing was, Franco also was checking for the white heel. We were going to meet after school in the gym locker room and exchange notes, but for now I had to remember what Shane had said: "Keep your eyes glued to the ground." As I did that I kept my ears open and heard, "Did you guys hear about the fire?"

I looked up and it was Kevin Whelan. His father was the chief of the Belltown fire department.

"I heard engines last night. What happened?" asked a girl I didn't know who was opening her locker.

"There was a big fire in the woods by the clearing near Coolidge Cranberry Bogs."

"How'd it start?" another kid asked.

"My dad thinks someone set it."

"Why would someone set a fire *there*?" the kids asked.

"I have no idea, except that they found a portrait of

Adolf Hitler hidden in the woods. He thinks it must be some sort of hate group."

The cat is out of the bag, I thought, as I tried to move closer to eavesdrop. I figured by third block it would be all around the school.

"A hate group? No. Not in our town," the girl said.

"Well, they also found torches and a white sheet."

"Wow, really? Do they have any suspects?" the girl asked.

Kevin scanned the area to see if anyone was listening, and I pretended I was tying my shoes.

"My dad found a small camera, like the kind you see in the James Bond movies."

My spy camera! I dropped my spy camera, too! I screamed in my head.

"He told me he found the camera right where they think the fire started in that gigantic briar patch. Of course, the camera is ruined, but whoever they trace it to is probably the person who started the fire."

I loved that camera. I shook my head and tied my laces.

"Well, I'd like to thank whoever started it," one of the kids said.

"Why?" Kevin asked.

"Well, now we don't have to take the shortcut through the briar patch if we want to go across town. Do you know how many times I've cut myself on the way to the movies?"

They all laughed because everyone seemed to have had a similar experience. I didn't laugh because I still felt the pain from my experience as I stood up and headed for the pay phone. I had to call Shane and clear my name before I became a suspect.

Shane's secretary answered and informed me that Shane had just returned from Boston and headed straight to the scene of last night's fire. She put me through to his voice mail: "Shane, I have some extremely important information. I have to take the late bus home, so meet me at my bus stop after school."

I hung up and tried to rub my eyes awake, but my lack of sleep was suddenly catching up to me.

"Oh, man, it's not even first period," I said to myself as I made my way into homeroom, knowing it was going to be a long day.

By third period my prediction came true. Everyone had heard about the fire, the white sheet, and Adolf Hitler portrait. What was worse were the whispers about me. They were beginning to get louder, especially since I looked like someone who had just been through a fire. I tried to ignore them and knew after I talked with Shane that I wanted my undercover days to end. After all, I didn't fool the enemy so why keep the charade going for my classmates, especially Gina? I made a vow that the first time I spotted her, I was going to force her to listen to me.

Unfortunately, shortly after I made that vow, I overheard Sandra Vincent say something about Gina being home sick in bed. Franco's and my behavior probably brought that on, I thought as I sat in the school library trying to stay focused on a book. But my eyes began to cross and the words got bigger and smaller and finally my eyelids fell. I was gone. Dead to the world, my dad would've said. I was dreaming about Vanessa and me at her birthday party when suddenly, "Wake up, Mr. Jacques!" The voice jarred me awake. When I opened my eyes, I saw Mrs. Willderly, the school librarian, staring down at me.

"Agh, you're not Vanessa," I blurted, causing a table of girls to break into hysterical laughter.

"No, I'm not, Mr. Jacques, this is a library! Not a lounge! I thought your library period already ended."

"What do you mean?" I said, but then noticed the clock on the wall.

"Oh, man!" I bolted past her and out the door. I couldn't believe it, but I had slept through the bell. On this day, the one class I didn't want to arrive late to was history.

When I slunk into class Mr. Kapulka was drawing something on the board, but stopped when he heard whispers behind him. "Orville, let's see." He looked down at his watch. "You're twenty minutes late, but you probably have a pass."

"No, I don't," I said, and I could hear the standard "Uh-oh" comments behind me.

He stared at me for a minute. "OK, well, see me after class."

"Busted!" someone shouted, and the class laughed.

"Nice face." And there was more laughter. Of course, it was Miller. He still hadn't thought up any new material.

"C'mon, class let's get back to our discussion." Mr. Kapulka pointed his chalk at the board while I tried to take my regular seat. Everyone in that area waved me away. Sue Edward smiled and pointed to the seat beside her. I sat down and Sue whispered, "Finally, someone who is on my side."

My stomach turned, but I forced a smile. "What are they talking about?"

"More of that Holocaust fantasy. Now they're saying Hitler was an evil person. My dad says ..." Sue began, but the class shushed her. If they had only heard what she was whispering they probably would have done worse.

"Sue, could you please keep it down so I can continue? Then if you have a viewpoint you will be more than welcome to give it," Mr. Kapulka said.

"Yeah, whatever." Sue rolled her eyes.

"Mr. Kapulka, you don't have to put up with ..." Wayne Rose began.

Mr. Kapulka waved his hand. "Please, Wayne. Let's get back to the subject."

I looked over at Sue and was amazed that nothing seemed to faze her. She wasn't paying any attention to Wayne's anger. Being Cape Verdean, this stuff really bothered Wayne. In fact, it bothered every other student who had a brain. But not Sue Edward! She was actually replacing her red press-on fingernails as Mr. Kapulka drew a cross on the board.

"Now, if you bend the cross here. Here. Here and here." He moved the chalk and the cross suddenly formed into a swastika.

"A swastika is really a crooked cross," he said and looked around for reactions.

"More like a twisted cross," Wayne said.

"What do you mean, Wayne?"

"The type of people who worship that stuff are twisted. Really twisted." Wayne stared over at Sue and me and shook his head in disappointment.

After class, Mr. Kapulka gave me a quick lecture on tardiness, but held off giving me a detention. He just ended the conversation with a concerned look. "Orville, it seems to me that you're very upset about something. You're not yourself these past couple of days. If you ever need someone to talk to, my door is always open."

I thanked Mr. Kapulka and spent the rest of the day fighting sleep until the final bell rang. My mind went over the order of things I had to do: Meet Franco in the locker room; meet Shane at my bus stop; meet the sandman!

"There was one other thing," I said to myself as I opened the locker room door. "What was it?"

"What was what?" said a voice behind me. I turned and expected Franco. It wasn't.

"Well, well, well," Paul Miller giggled.

"Miller, what's the deal? Are you following me?" I asked, and this time I was a little nervous, because we were alone.

"Don't flatter yourself, Jacques. It was just a coincidence. But ..." Miller popped his head out the doorway and checked to see if the coast was clear. Apparently it was, because he shut the door and laughed. "What a wonderful coincidence it was, though."

"What do you mean?" I asked, even though I knew exactly what he meant.

"I've been waiting a while to get you alone so we can settle a few things. You think I forgot about how your girl-friend jumped Craig and me at the carnival?" He pushed me. He was referring to an incident that happened at Belltown Winter Carnival, which of course, he provoked.

"Hey, you guys started that."

He ignored my comment and pushed again. "And then how you tried to make me look bad yesterday in history. That sure backfired on you."

I tried to push back but I could hear my voice stutter a bit. "I just repeated what … ah … you… said."

"It's funny, Jacques. This morning you were all laughs. You're not laughing now, are you?" Miller cocked his arm back and was about to throw a punch when the locker room door flew open.

"Hey Orville, are you in here?" Franco hollered.

"I'm right here, Franco." I smiled as Franco appeared and Miller put his arm down.

"Am I interrupting something?" Franco's eyebrows raised.

"No, nothing at all. The more the merrier. Right, Miller?" My confidence was soaring now with Franco, the offensive lineman, for my back up.

"Nothing's going on, Dan." Miller didn't dare call him Franco. That name was just meant for friends.

"I don't know. It looks like something is going on to me. Is he bothering you, Orville?" Franco moved closer and now Miller was the one backing up.

"No, don't worry about it, Franco. Miller was just leav-ing. Right, Miller?" I stressed.

"Yeah, I just gotta get some stuff out of my locker." Miller went over to his locker and spun the dial.

Franco grinned at me and then asked in a low voice, "Any luck on you-know-what?"

"No. How about you?"

"Nothing, O man. The only thing I learned was some people in this school wear some pretty nasty footwear." Franco and I laughed and Miller looked over to see what was so humorous. "Hey, Miller. Hurry up and get out of here before I lose my good mood," Franco barked and then gave me another grin. He was enjoying putting a little fear into the school bully.

"I'm almost done." Miller opened a duffle bag and fired some clothes into it. We were about to turn our attention back to our conversation when we both noticed Miller pulling something else out of his gym locker—a pair of Cape Adventurer boots covered with paint spots. I felt my chest flutter with excitement.

"Orville! Look!" Franco pointed.

"I know! I know! Miller, are those your boots?"

For a second Miller forgot Franco was around. "What a stupid question that is." Then Miller felt Franco's glare. "I mean, yeah. Why?"

"Because ..." Franco began, and I shot him a stern glance of Franco-this-is-not-the-time. He caught it and nodded in agreement.

"I was just wondering," I said nonchalantly. "They looked like a pair of boots I lost."

"Well, they're not." Miller threw the boots into his bag and zipped it up. He deliberately bumped me as he passed.

"Jacques,   I'll see you later."

"Yeah, later, Miller." I said and smiled at Franco. I knew the next time Miller would see me was after Detective Shane O'Connell interrogated him about the hate crimes he committed. Paul Miller was a small fish in this case, and we couldn't risk blowing everything by forcing the issue. I was confident that he would flail away and fry under the interrogation lights. I was sure by the end of the day, Miller would lead the Belltown Police to the biggest fish of them all, the leader of the Sons of Hitler, the face behind the scarlet sheet.

CHAPTER
SEVEN

I HAD BEEN waiting at my bus stop for close to an hour and was about to go home when Shane's minivan slipped around the corner. He pulled up and then reached over and pushed open the passenger door. "Orville, jump in but watch out for the tray." He pointed to a cardboard carrying tray holding two Styrofoam cups of coffee.

"Can you grab mine? It's on the left. The other one is yours. Light. Lots of sugar, right?"

"Yup, thanks." I said and handed Shane his cup. We both took quick sips of the steaming coffee and said in unison, "ahhhh." Shane put his cup in the pullout holder beneath the dash and shifted the car into drive.

"The coffee is my way of saying, sorry I'm late. I got ambushed by that new reporter for the *Belltown News*, Eve Capshaw."

"Oh, no problem." I said and took another sip.

"She said she wanted to ask me about last night's fire, and then she threw all these stats at me about crime in Belltown having gone up twenty percent in the last two years. She then asked, 'Why is the Belltown Police Department failing?' How do you answer something like that? The woman had me all flustered. I thought I was on '60 Minutes.'"

"Yeah, that's Eve for ya. I wouldn't be surprised if someday she ends up working as an investigative reporter for *Time* or someplace."

"Yup. She's something else." Shane gave a little smile to himself.

Hmmm, I wondered if there was another reason Eve had him flustered. I think Shane felt my curious stare because he abruptly said, "Enough about her. I guess you had quite a night at the little campfire by the clearing."

"I didn't mention I was there in my message to you. How did you know?"

"First off, the bandages on your face," he said, while keeping his eyes on the road.

"Oh, yeah." I felt my bandages. I had forgotten that I still had them on.

"Also, check under the seat."

I looked under my seat and pulled out a plastic bag containing my melted spy camera.

"Fire Chief Whelan found it. I paid good money for that camera. I hope it wasn't a complete waste. What did you find out last night?"

"A lot. But I just found out even more."

"Like what?" Shane pushed.

"Like the name of the person who can bring you to their leader." I smiled in satisfaction.

"Their leader? What are you talking about? Whose leader?" He asked as he pulled over to the side of the road.

I gave him a serious look. "The Sons of Hitler, Shane. This is no longer about some ignorant kid. This is about a hate movement. A hate movement growing right here in Belltown. And Shane, we have to stop it. Now."

Even though it was my little sister Jackie's turn for kitchen duty, Mom looked at me and then pointed at the dirty dishes. I didn't say a word. I just began clearing the table. That was Mom's way of saying that she was suspicious of my behavior, and well, she had every right to be. Earlier, when I came to the dinner table, I made a major blunder by not being prepared for her obvious question, "Orville, what happened to your face?" I was speechless for a few seconds, but finally came up with this lame response.

"I . . . I know Dad and you don't want me to begin shaving until I'm a little older, but I thought I'd give it a try."

"Really? Well, where did you get the razor?"

"I . . . ah . . . bought it at the store."

"I see. Well, this is one reason why we didn't want you to start shaving. Your face isn't ready for it yet."

"Mom, I promise I won't do it again." I really believed my excuse worked.

"One other thing to remember, Orville, when you do

start to shave. Don't shave there." She pointed at the bandage stuck to my forehead. Mom didn't say anything else. That was when I knew she hadn't bought it, and I would either have to come clean with the truth or get stuck with kitchen duty. There was no choice, but I really didn't mind doing the dishes. It gave me time to sort out everything in my mind. First, I thought about Shane's reaction to my information. He had mixed feelings. He was thrilled with what I uncovered on Paul Miller: the Scarlet Man, the blue pick-up truck with the license plate beginning with the letter P, the group's name— the Sons of Hitler. But what caused him great concern was he felt Rabbi Spielman and he had totally underestimated the magnitude of what had been going on in Belltown. The last thing he said as he dropped me off was, "We should have made our information public from day one."

Should'ves, could'ves, would'ves, I thought as I washed an unbelievably greasy pan. How were they to know that it was far worse than they both had imagined? After all, one of the first incidents that occurred was with Hitler's name being misspelled. So, how were they to know that had come from a hate group that actually worshipped Hitler? Shane was also a little apprehensive about telling his Chief how he got his information. I insisted he not mention my name, and he agreed, knowing his job would be on the line if the truth came out about my involvement in the case.

"It will be over soon enough," I whispered, thinking of Miller selling out his leader for a lighter punishment. As I scrubbed the next pan, my mind shifted to Vanessa and her upcoming surprise party. Then it clicked.

"Oh, man, the jewelry store. That's what I forgot." I remembered that if I wanted to buy the "perfect gift" for Vanessa, I was supposed to go to the jewelry store that afternoon. I looked up at the wall clock—7:15.

"Too late." I'll go by there tomorrow, I decided, when the phone rang in the family room. I rushed to it, but Mom had beaten me there.

"Yes, Orville is right here. May I ask who's calling?" Mom paused and then gave me a strange look. "Oh hello, Rabbi Spielman . . . Yes . . . Yes . . . I know your wife . . . Yes, we should get together sometime . . . I will . . . The moment my husband returns from Ireland . . . Yes . . . Yes . . . I do miss him terribly, but it was a once in a lifetime opportunity. OK . . . Yes, good talking to you, too," Mom passed me the phone and even though she didn't have to, she said, "It's Rabbi Spielman."

"Thanks," I grabbed the phone. "Hello."

Rabbi Spielman skipped the greeting. "Your Mom probably wouldn't invite us over if she knew the danger I put you in."

"Correct," I said because Mom was still in the room.

The Rabbi understood. "I probably shouldn't have called at your house, but there was no answer at The Shack, and I wanted to talk to you tonight."

Mom was pretending to stay busy flipping through some bills, but I knew her curiosity was taking hold of her. She was trying to do some serious eavesdropping and I got an idea.

"Yes, Rabbi. Yes, about your case."

Mom turned around quickly.

"I did find your dog, but I got caught in a thorn bush chasing him. Excuse me for a second." I put my hand on the phone for dramatics and turned to Mom.

"Mom, I'm sorry. I didn't cut my face shaving. I was working on this dog case. I didn't mean to lie to you, but I knew you didn't want me to do any more investigative stuff."

Mom smiled in spite of herself. "You should have told me the truth, but help the Rabbi find his dog. I'll give you some privacy." Mom shut the door and I kind of felt bad because I lied to her, but I rationalized a bit. At least I told her about being cut by a thorn bush. I knew that would never pass if it came up for parental review!

"OK, Rabbi. Shoot."

"Shane told me everything, and I just want to thank you for risking your life last night."

"No problem. What's next?"

"As we speak, Shane is probably talking to the young man, and he is confident there will be a confession that will lead us to the real source of the problem: the man who was wearing that scarlet sheet."

"Yeah, Shane could make a mute talk."

He gave a light laugh. "I did make a horrible mistake thinking it was one or a couple of young people, though. I am going to grant Miss Capshaw an interview tomorrow afternoon to inform the people of Belltown what really has been going on."

"That's a good idea."

"As for you, Orville, I want to settle the bill. What do I owe you for your work?"

"Nothing, Rabbi. Just knowing that Belltown will be safe from these sickos is good enough payment."

"I thought you'd say that. So, I'm giving you a week to think up the proper payment. I'm serious, Orville. Work on a bill for me. Well, I'd better get to the police station. I want to sit down with this young man and get to the core of his anger and educate him, and maybe, just maybe, he will turn into a good citizen in our town. Good night, Orville."

"Goodnight, Rabbi," I hung up.

If Rabbi Spielman could work miracles and turn Paul Miller into a good kid, that would be my ultimate payment. But as I headed back into the kitchen, something told me even the caring Rabbi couldn't pull off that miracle!

The next day everyone on my school bus sat in silence, but that was always the case in the morning. It was an unwritten law not to speak. We would always sit trancelike and enjoy the last few minutes of not having to use our brains! But when the bus stopped to pick up Rob Kubicheck, everyone let out a faint groan of sadness. It wasn't because we didn't like Rob. In fact, everyone seemed to like him. We groaned because he was our last passenger pick up, and that meant the next time the doors swung open we would have to get up out of our seats and head off to face another tedious day at Belltown High School. I think that's the reason that when our bus driver, Mr. Norris, came to a stop and cranked the door handle, we automatically rose to our feet and began walking down the aisle, unaware of our surroundings.

"Everyone, get back in your seats," Mr. Norris ordered, as Officer Warner entered the bus. I glanced out the window and realized that we weren't even close to school. It was probably another two miles away and the road leading to it was blocked by a cruiser with flashing blue and white lights.

"Sorry, Mr. Norris, but you can't take this road. I guess they didn't tell you that it's probably going to be closed all day."

"No one told me anything." Mr. Norris looked annoyed.

By now everyone was awake and Rob asked, "Why's the road closed, Officer Warner?"

Officer Warner was about to answer when he spotted a truck behind our bus. "Wait one second. I have to let this truck through." He jumped from the steps and waved the truck around us. As it passed, I noticed it had a satellite dish attached to it. Someone shouted, "Hey, you guys. That's a news truck." As the truck whizzed by I was barely able to make out the lettering—Channel 7 Boston.

"There must have been a major car accident to have a Boston news truck come down to the Cape," Mr. Norris said, and we all nodded in agreement.

"It wasn't a car accident," Officer Warner said as he mounted the steps again.

"What was it?" everyone asked at the same time.

"Some vandals hit the Belltown Cemetery last night."

"But the Belltown Cemetery is on the other side of town," Mr. Norris said.

"Oh yeah, I should have said they hit the Belltown *Jewish* Cemetery down the road."

"What!" I heard myself yell.

"Yeah. They destroyed the place. It looks like a battlefield. Speaking of battlefields, I better get back to my post. See you later, Mr. Norris."

"Yes. Goodbye, Officer Warner." Mr. Norris waved goodbye to Warner and then spied me in his mirror as I was rushing down the aisle.

"Orville, get back in your seat."

"I can't," was all I said as I ran past him and jumped down the steps.

"Orville!" he yelled, and then leaned on his horn a couple of times. Officer Warner turned around and Mr. Norris pointed in my direction.

"Hey, come back here! You're not supposed to go down that road!" Warner yelled, but I knew he couldn't chase me because that would mean leaving his post. After going about three hundred yards, I came to the entrance of the Belltown Jewish Cemetery. It was amazing how a few minutes earlier, I was barely awake and silence had surrounded me. It was complete chaos now. There were media trucks and cruisers parked everywhere. I spotted a crowd of reporters force-feeding their microphones to the chief of Police, and a pensive-looking Shane O'Connell. I wanted to run over to Shane and shake him and ask, Why did this happen again? This wasn't supposed to happen! It was supposed to be over! But I continued walking on towards the cemetery. I came upon another reporter getting ready to talk to the camera so I stopped for a second. She was a pretty woman, whom I recognized from TV, but I didn't know her name. She stared into the camera. "We all know the postcard scenery of Belltown, Cape Cod, but this morning this town learned that not everything it has to offer is beautiful. I am here at the Belltown Jewish Cemetery where last night unidentified vandals made this ah … ah … oh, man. I messed up, Johnny. Let's try another take.

And remember, when I finish speaking, I want you to pan over and focus on that crying girl over there. Can your camera pick her up clearly from this distance? I don't want her to know we're shooting her." She pointed over to a girl in a red winter coat in the distance huddled in front of a gravestone.

"It's pretty far, but this camera can get anything. She won't have a clue I'm shooting her until she watches the six o'clock news." The cameraman smiled and began to adjust the camera's lens.

"Beautiful. That will give this piece that extra punch of drama that the other channels can only dream of." The reporter gave a satisfied laugh and then cleared her throat. A sharp wave of anger hit the pit of my stomach at their lack of compassion. I squinted to focus on the girl in the red coat. Something about her looked familiar. As the reporter began speaking again, I squinted harder and was barely able to identify the girl, but I did—Gina!

" . . . but not everything about this town is beautiful. I am . . ." The reporter was in mid-sentence and didn't see me as I lunged over and snatched the cordless microphone out of her hands and fired it out into the street.

"What the . . . What are you crazy?" the reporter yelled at me.

"What's wrong with you?!" the cameraman followed.

"No, what's wrong with *you*?" I yelled back and took off into the cemetery. Up close and personal, it was a hundred times worse. Tombstones were toppled, cracked in half, or desecrated with maroon spray-painted swastikas, or hate comments. This was supposed to have ended last night, I thought, as I shook with anger. Miller was supposed to have talked.

Officer Warner was right, I thought. The cemetery did look like a battlefield. Except in a battle there are always two sides fighting. In this war, the Sons of Hitler had done all the fighting and their enemies were people who could no longer breathe, never mind fight back. It was almost impossible for me to hold in my emotions as I approached Gina. I think I had seen her cry once before, and those were tears from laughing too hard. In fact, that was what Gina Goldman was known for, laughing or making other people laugh. But now she was crying and the sight looked unreal. Except it *was* real and there was nothing I could do as she squatted, hugging a tombstone that had been sledgehammered in half.

"Gina." It was the only word I could utter. She swung her head around and her red eyes glared at me for a second before she let go of the stone and stood up. She frantically wiped her eyes dry before pointing to the stone and asking, "Do you know who this is?" There was a lone tear still trickling down the side of her face, and I wanted desperately to wipe it away, but I had to remain cautious because of her untrusting eyes.

"No. I don't know who that is," I had to admit. The name was illegible due to the maroon swastika in the middle of the remaining stone.

"That's my grandmother."

"The grandmother who only had the ...ah ..." I stopped.

"One arm. Yes, you might remember her for having one arm, but I just remember her for being the best grandmother in the world. Nana Goldman."

"Yes, Nana Goldman. I remember her now," I said softly, thinking of Gina's grandmother whom everyone knew as

Nana. Gina once told me that Nana had lost her right arm in a childhood accident that Nana never talked about, but her disability never seemed strange to me when I was little. She was just a loving grandmother who would often spoil us with hot chocolate and oven-baked cookies after we had been sledding down the hill in her backyard. Nana Goldman died when we were around eight years old.

Gina slumped back down and hopelessly tried putting the pieces of crushed rock back together. I took her hand. "Gina, we'll get Nana Goldman a new stone."

She shouted back. "Why! So they can do it again?! Why would anyone do this? Don't they have a Nana?! How would they like it if I did this to them!" Gina clutched the crushed rock in disgust.

"Gina, I'm so sorry. I . . ."

Gina's anger at me suddenly dawned on her. "Sorry! Orville, how would you like it if I did this to you!" She shook her hand as if to throw the rock at me but then threw it to the ground and collapsed. I got on my knees and put my arms around her as she sobbed. "Why, Orville? You're just like them. You're just like them."

I put my hands on her arms and looked into her eyes. "Listen to me, Gina. I've been trying to help."

"Trying to help?" She began pushing me away.

"That's part of the problem, Gina. You won't listen to me. I've been working on this as a case."

"What?" She was dumbfounded.

"Gina, Orville is telling the truth." Rabbi Spielman rushed over to us.

"What are you talking about, Rabbi? Orville said . . ." Gina's voice was mixed with tears and confusion.

"I hired Orville to work undercover for me. This isn't the first time this has happened. He was working on this case, and what a fool I was to let him. This whole thing has jeopardized your friendship—not to mention Orville's life." The Rabbi scolded himself as he helped us both to our feet.

"Oh, my. Why didn't you tell me, Orville? You promised to always let me in on your cases!" Gina was furious again, and in a way her anger was strangely comforting because at least she now knew the truth.

"Gina, I messed up. I should have told you, but when I realized that, it was too late. I tried to tell you, but you wouldn't talk to me."

"Hey, don't make me the bad one here," Gina snapped and then we were both silent for a minute. I wanted to say, Maybe if you had a little more faith in our friendship you would have let me explain everything. But I kept my mouth shut.

"Well, do you have any suspects?" she asked coldly.

"Yes. I know Paul Miller is involved, and Shane was going to question him last night. In fact, I don't know why this happened. This whole case should have been solved last night."

"Paul Miller. Well, that doesn't shock me. I never liked . . ." Gina began, but the Rabbi interrupted.

"Hold on a minute, Orville."

"Rabbi, in view of everything, I think Gina deserves to know the truth."

"I agree. She does, Orville, but Paul Miller has nothing to do with it." Rabbi Spielman shook his head.

"What are you talking about?" I asked, shocked.

"He's talking about Paul Miller's alibi," Shane said as he approached us.

"What about it, Shane?" I couldn't believe what I was hearing.

"Paul Miller has an air-tight alibi. He had nothing to do with any of the hate crimes."

"Then who does, Detective?" Gina asked.

Shane looked long and hard around at the destruction in the cemetery and then said, "I wish I could answer that question, Gina. I really do."

At that moment, I made a vow that no matter what danger lay ahead, I would find an answer to Gina's question, or at least go to my own grave trying.

CHAPTER
EIGHT

I HAD BEEN waiting for Shane in his minivan for about twenty minutes and I still didn't know what Paul Miller had used for an alibi. Shane was going to tell us, when we were interrupted by the reporter and cameraman, cursing and demanding to press charges against me. With everything Shane had to deal with, I felt bad that he now had spent precious time trying to talk them out of filing a report. He looked weary as he climbed into his minivan, grabbed his radio, and informed dispatch he was dropping off a student at Belltown High. I sensed he was angry and I knew it was probably at me, so I waited for him to talk. Finally, he said, "They're not going to press charges."

"Oh, thanks Shane. I'm sorry. I know you're mad at me, but I just got so angry when I saw how they were going to invade Gina's privacy."

"Orville, I'm far from mad at you. Some of those media people are callous individuals. Anyway, Orville, you're the only one who has found out anything solid. If I'm mad at anyone, it's myself. I've done a lousy job on this one."

I was relieved to find out that Shane wasn't mad at me, and I knew that was my cue to say, "Yeah, but I messed up with Paul Miller. I thought for sure with the paint on his boots that he was our guy. Hey, what was his alibi, anyway?"

"I almost jumped the gun myself when I saw his boots. But always remember what I told you—not everything is always what it appears to be. Paul Miller's father is a house painter. Sometimes after school, Miller works for his dad to make a few extra bucks. With that info, put together with solid alibis, including one placing Miller at a wedding anniversary party up in Boston the night the Stein's barn was vandalized, the kid is clean. Paul Miller is only guilty of being an unlikable bully, and unfortunately I can't charge him for that." Shane turned the wheel and we headed down School Street.

Shane nodded to himself. "Yup, I'm gonna take a lot of heat for this one. Not only did they hit the cemetery last night, they also cleaned out six summer houses."

"What?"

"Yeah, six summer houses were broken into last night."

"How do you know the Sons of Hitler did it? Did they spray paint swastikas?"

"No, that's the one thing that bothers me, and I don't exactly know if they were the ones. But my gut says they were involved because of other evidence. Orville, are you up for a little detective quiz?" Shane forced a smile.

"Sure, fire away."

"At three AM dispatch received a 911 call from a female. They couldn't tell if the female was old or young. Anyway, the caller said that she was looking out of her bedroom window and saw that there was a group of people at the Belltown Jewish Cemetery breaking gravestones. So, naturally, in view of everything going on, dispatch didn't even hesitate and sent all available cars. In three minutes, the cruisers were at the cemetery, but the crime had already been committed and there was no one to be found. Meanwhile, the rest of Belltown was left unguarded and they cleaned out six summerhouses. Granted, we were pretty stupid to send all available cars, but we're only talking about five cruisers at that time of night. That's the problem with lack of police protection in a growing community like Belltown." He sounded like he was addressing the Belltown Board of Selectman.

"I still don't get it," I said. "It might be a coincidence that both these things happened the same night, and the guys got away before the cruisers got there. What about the woman who saw it from her house? What did she say? Did she see where they went? What they were driving—like a blue pickup?" I drilled him with questions.

Shane actually laughed. "Well, I guess you flunked the quiz. Orville, do you sleep on your school bus when you ride to school or something?"

I had to laugh. "Actually, I do. Why?"

"Because there are no houses within two miles of the Belltown Jewish Cemetery. So how could this female, who we think *might* be young by her voice, how could she have seen these people out of her bedroom window?"

"Oh, man." It sank in.

"Yup, that's what I said. They set us up. They knew we would be so gung-ho to catch them that we would send everybody. They burned us twice last night, and it's driving me crazy," Shane said as I opened the car door.

"We'll get them, Shane."

"I hate to say this, Orville, but there is no 'we' anymore. The deal was if this got dangerous you'd get out of it, and this is far beyond dangerous, buddy. I'm sorry."

I gritted my teeth. "I understand, Shane, but keep me posted. Hey, did you find anything on the blue truck and the plate?"

"We ran a check and there are 13 thousand blue trucks that have Massachusetts plates that begin with P. Out of those, fifteen hundred and sixty something of them are Cape trucks. None in Belltown, but it does narrow the search down for us."

"Yeah, but not enough. I guess I got cut up in those thorn bushes for nothing," I said, dejected.

"No, you're wrong about that. We found out that the Sons of Hitler is a hate group that is growing nationally. They describe themselves as a combination of skinheads and Ku Klux Klan, but they claim they have a direct line to Hitler—that he actually communicates with them. Many believe they began in a small town in Arizona. So, don't think your work was for nothing because if we can pin down their leader in Arizona, we might be able to pin down their leader here. See you later, Orville. And thanks again for getting off the case."

"No problem," I said and shut the door with one hand. The other hand was behind my back with two fingers crossed.

I stood staring out The Shack window waiting for Gina to pick me up, but my mind was elsewhere. It had been a tragic morning for Belltown, and my day hadn't been much better. My homeroom teacher gave me a note from Miss Turner, my Driver's Ed. teacher. It notified me that since I skipped my driving the day before, I wouldn't have privileges to finish my required driving for at least three weeks! I only had a couple more hours of driving left and then I'd be able to go for my license. Now I would have to wait another three weeks to finish. To me, that was a lifetime away. I had looked for Miss Turner so I could explain that I had just plain forgotten, but as my luck had it she was at a Driver's Ed. conference on the dangers of drunk driving off campus. In algebra, Mr. Reasons gave us a test, which I knew I flagged shortly after I put my name on the paper. In history, everyone was still giving me the cold shoulder, and then to top off everything, my guidance counselor cornered me at the end of the school day and suggested we meet sometime soon to discuss my dropping grades. Yup, it had been a lousy day, but I figured it could get much worse. After all, there were some positives. One was Gina. She hadn't gone to school because she was emotionally drained, so I had gone to her house to clear the air. We had a long talk and although she still seemed a little angry, she forgave me. And then I told her about Franco's help in the case. Her eyes brightened up, but her mood was guarded. All she said was, "He left a message on my machine saying something like that. I suppose I will have to return his call now."

The other positive involved Gina picking me up to go to a town rally that school and town officials began organizing moments after the vandalism at the Belltown Jewish Cemetery. At this rally, Vanessa Hyde was planning to meet me, and that was the biggest positive of all. I had called her that afternoon and told her a little about the case and promised to tell the rest the next time I saw her. It was her suggestion to meet at the rally.

"Oh no. The jewelry store," I suddenly blurted out. I had forgotten again about the "perfect gift" I was supposed to buy Vanessa for her birthday at the jewelry store. Maybe Gina can drive me by the store first, I thought, as I spotted Gina's truck approaching. When I read the 911 on the side of the vehicle, I realized it wasn't her truck at all. It was an ambulance. I knew it was Mr. Lopes, an EMT who lived up the street. As the numbers 911 slowly rolled by something hit me! "A female's voice! Why didn't I think of that earlier?" I said to myself. It was probably because of all the distractions in school that I wasn't able to focus on the case, I rationalized. But standing alone staring out The Shack window my mind was free to think and something Shane had said stuck in my head. It was so obvious, but I hadn't thought of it before—the person who made the 911 call was a female. A female was in on it. Shane had said the police weren't sure but the caller sounded young. I thought back to the history class that day. Sue Edward, who was hardly ever absent, had been. Why? "Wouldn't you stay home from school if you had been up at three in the morning making phone calls?" I asked myself with a smile. When I had found out that the hate group was called the Sons of

Hitler, I had naturally crossed Sue Edward off my list. But now there was proof a female was involved in the group. Even if the female's part was to make a phone call to the police at three in the morning. I rushed over to my detective journal and turned to the page titled "List of Suspects," where Sue Edward's name was on the page, crossed out. As Gina honked her horn, I took my pencil and quickly erased the line through Sue Edward's name. I had a suspect again, and that was better than anything. Well, except for one thing—proof. What I needed now was some concrete proof to show that Sue Edward was involved, and as the horn honked again, I got an idea of just how I was going to get it.

I wasn't going to keep any more secrets from Gina so I told her my theory on Sue Edward.

"It's certainly not out in left field," Gina said. "I wouldn't be surprised if she was involved. I would love it if we could bust her. She's a cruel person. I wonder why some people are so mean?"

"Hey, Gina, before I forget again, can we stop by that fancy jewelry store on Main Street?" I asked.

Gina's face clouded instantly. "No."

"What?"

"No. I mean, I'm . . . it's after five, it's probably closed."

"I think it's open till six tonight."

"We'll be late for the . . ." she began.

"Don't worry, it'll only take me a second. I just have to

look at a birthday gift for Vanessa because . . ."

"Orville, don't you get it! I don't want to go there!" Gina erupted. I put my hands up, "Hold on, Gina. I know it's been a hard day on you and you're still angry, but that doesn't give you the right to bite my head off whenever you feel like it."

Gina pulled over to the side of the road. I wasn't sure if she was about to throw me out of her truck or something. She took a long breath. "You're right, Orville. I'm sorry. It's just that in the past week or so I have found out things I never knew before and it has affected me strongly."

I wanted to say, "Like how you were so quick to judge me," but I held my tongue and listened.

"Like yesterday, Orville. Since Nana Goldman died when I was eight, back then I never dared ask how. Yesterday I did. That is when my parents gave me the letter. And then out of the blue you bring up the jewelry store on Main Street. I'm sorry, it just rattled me."

"I don't understand. What does the jewelry store have to do with it?" I asked.

"My parents told me that Nana Goldman was buying me a birthday gift in that store when she had a sudden stroke and died."

Boy, I thought, can't I say anything right?

"Well, of course, when my parents told me, I got upset thinking maybe if Nana hadn't been out buying me a gift she wouldn't have had a stroke." Gina looked away from me and pulled the truck back onto the road.

"Gina, you know that's ridiculous," I said.

"I know. I really do, but sometimes you can't help feeling that guilt and asking the 'what if' questions."

"You know, I can relate to that," I said, thinking of my friend Will who died while I was working on a case. I often wondered if maybe he'd still be alive if I hadn't investigated the Cranberry Beach murder. "But you can't think that," I said.

"You're right. And now my parents are all upset that they told me. Anyway, I hope you can understand why I flew off the handle when you mentioned that jewelry store. Just a coincidence that got my feelings all worked up."

I wanted to change the subject, and I wasn't sure if this was the right move, but I figured my luck couldn't get any worse. "Speaking of feelings, have you talked to Franco?"

Gina broke into a mischievous smile. "I did. But, no matter what good intentions he had, he did lie to me. I can't have that. So, let's just say Mr. Daniel Francais will have to sweat a bit before I completely forgive him." She laughed and I joined in.

Gina faked a serious expression. "That goes for you, too, Mr. Jacques."

"Oh, believe me, I know Miss Goldman. I'm sweating it." I laughed and she couldn't help but join in. It was a wonderful feeling to laugh with my good friend again, and for the next ten minutes, we did just that, laugh like normal teenagers. We were going to savor this moment, because we both knew our laughter wouldn't last long.

Gina and I didn't say anything to each other as we stood waiting in a long line outside the Belltown High School auditorium. Of course, even if we wanted to talk, we probably wouldn't have heard one another. Everyone in line was chatting feverishly about the vandalism in the cemetery. We were both content eavesdropping on the conversations around us as the line inched forward at snail-speed. One conversation caught both our ears. "I can't believe this happened in our town!" one elderly woman said to her blue-haired friend.

"I know, Gertrude. I'm sorry to say, but I think it was a group of young people."

"No question in my mind, Mildred. I never thought I'd hear myself say this, but kids today are nothing but trouble. And I think this whole thing stems from that MTV and music they listen to. Nothing but garbage."

The elderly woman named Mildred let out a good-natured laugh and turned around to us. "Did you kids hear that?" We politely nodded as she continued, "When Miss Proper over here was your age she used to be head-over-heels for ol' blue eyes Frank Sinatra and his music. Whenever she did anything bad, her mother would blame it on Sinatra's music. Gertrude, you know what? You've become your mother."

"Oh, hush now." Gertrude swatted her hand, but smiled in spite of herself.

Mildred turned her attention from us back to Gertrude. "Gert, there is nothing wrong with children today. Children will always be children. It's the people who are raising the children. That's the problem. They're using the same old destructive ideas that they were taught. They don't seem to learn from history that we are all connected."

Gina gave me a tug on my jacket as if to say, I totally agree with her. I nodded back and was about to say how much

I also agreed when I spotted Vanessa and that smile of hers heading our way. My heart jumped a beat. I still wasn't used to the power of that smile, especially when it was flashing at me. I returned her smile with "Hey, Vanessa, what's up?"

"Hey, Orville. Hey, Gina. I've been looking for you guys. You don't have to wait in line. This line is for people who don't have seats. Kip and I already saved you guys seats right next to us."

I think Gina said, "Great," but I'm not quite sure. All I heard was "Kip and I." Whoa, where did this curveball come from? I wondered.

"Who's Kip?" I nervously asked, as we followed her into another door leading to the auditorium.

"Oh, he's a friend of mine. He goes to Belltown Academy with me. I think you'll really like him, Orville."

Oh yeah, I can tell he's my new best friend, I thought as a tall blond-haired kid got up and shook my hand with a tight grip. "Kip Taylor. You must be Orville."

"Ah, yeah. Good to meet you," I said, but I was thinking, Where did this joker come from? I needed to figure out what was going on, so I threw my coat on my seat and told them I had to use the bathroom. In the bathroom I splashed some water on my face and thought about this sudden turn of events. Vanessa said Kip was a friend? He could be just that— a friend. Why get so excited? Kip. What kind of a stupid name is that? I thought. Then my mind ordered—you can't think that way or you'll act that way. Vanessa will get angry if you act like a jealous jerk. Be nice. Be extra nice. They probably are just friends.

"Anyway, Orville is hardly a name to be proud of," I said

into the mirror as Scotty Donovan walked in. Normally, Scotty would have made a joke about me looking into the mirror, but his look told me he still thought the anti-Semitic rumors were true so he just said in monotone, "Hey, what's up?"

I tried to ignore his mood and said, "Hey, Scotty, I've been wanting to ask you something. Did you ever find out who donated the metal trunk? 'Cause I figure that person can tell you why it was so valuable and then …"

"Detective O'Halloran from the Silver Shore Police had the same theory, Orville. The problem is sometimes people just leave whatever they donate out in the back shed. That's what they did with the trunk. I remember I brought it in that morning, there was something… and now it's pretty strange …" Scotty stopped.

"What's pretty strange?" Even though I had been working on my own case, my curiosity about the metal trunk and Clark Harrison's death hadn't stopped.

"Nothing. I shouldn't even be talking to you. I heard what you said in history class. It wasn't cool." Before I could object, Scotty was gone. Even though Scotty's comment intrigued me, I forced myself to stop thinking about it. I stared into the mirror one last time and practiced my fake smile. "Kip, what an interesting name." Little did I know, in a few minutes, putting on a fake smile for Kip Taylor would be the least of my problems!

By the time I came back into the auditorium, the Chief had just finished addressing everyone about the situation, and was opening the floor for questions or comments. Wayne Rose was the first person in the crowd to grab the microphone. As Wayne stated his name, school, and year of graduation, I tried to slink unnoticed down the main aisle to my seat. No such luck as his eyes found mine, and when he paused for a second, our eyes locked. Finally, I looked away and he continued. "I would like to challenge any member of this Sons of Hitler group that the Chief talked about. I challenge them to look me in the eye face to face and tell me that I am a second-class citizen. I will not fight you, and maybe I will respect you a little more if you take off your trick-or-treat costumes and face me."

The auditorium was silent as Wayne waited and glanced over in my direction as I finally found my seat. Wayne's voice slowly rose, "You see, they will not come forward. They will only look at us through eyeholes. They will only attack people who cannot defend themselves. The Sons of Hitler are weak people. Are we going to allow weak people to ruin our community? I say, no! Tonight, we see that Belltown is hurting but we are still strong because we are here! By being here for our Jewish neighbors, we are here for every neighbor, because that is what makes this the greatest town on Cape Cod. We are a community. We are one! So pack your bags, Sons of Hitler, because there is no way you're going to ruin our town!" Wayne's voice hit the highest level, but then he calmly returned the mike to the stand. And at this point, he was the only calm person in the entire auditorium. I looked around and there were smiles of hope on everyone's face, including Gertrude and Mildred, who were two rows up from me to the right. I could tell by Mildred's mannerisms that she was pointing out that there were still good kids in this world and Gertrude was clapping and nodding enthusiastically. When the clapping finally quieted, I was about to sit down when my coat fell off my seat. As I picked it up a piece of paper fell out of my coat. I sat back down in my seat and unfolded the paper. It was a note:

Dear Orville,

I found out who the leader is. Meet me behind the school. Now. Alone.

Franco

P.S. No matter what, don't tell Gina

I looked around to see if Gina had seen me reading the letter. She was still talking to Vanessa and Kip telling them who Wayne was, since they went to Belltown Academy. I got up and the whole row looked a little annoyed, because everyone had to move their legs again so I could get by.

"Where are you going now?" Gina and Vanessa asked.

"My mouth is dry. I've got to get a drink."

They were about to say something when Mr. Finn, our principal, grabbed the microphone. "How do I follow that young man who exemplifies what is great about Belltown High. I just ..." Mr. Finn's voice faded as I made my way out of the auditorium door and went down the hall headed for the back of the school. Franco must have slipped the note into my coat when I was in the bathroom, I thought, as I opened the door and headed outside. I cupped my hands and half-shouted, "Franco, where are you?"

No one responded.

"He could have been more precise about where behind

the school he wanted to meet," I mumbled as I walked alondside the cafeteria windows. I glanced over at the window and gasped. "Ah, no!" Spray painted in maroon—*Hitler Rules!*

"Man, not again," I said in disgust as my foot kicked against something. I looked down and it was a can of spray paint. I reached down and slowly picked it up when suddenly out of nowhere a police cruiser appeared, blinding me with a floodlight. The loud speaker voice barked, "Drop it and get down on your stomach!"

"What?" I was stunned.

"Drop the can, now! Get down on all fours! Now!"

"But, wait. I can explain. I . . ."

"NOW! DO IT!"

I was trembling as I got onto my stomach. I tried talking, but the policeman yelled, "Keep quiet! You're under arrest for defacing school property. You have the right to remain silent . . ." I felt the cold cuffs lock around my wrists and the police officer thenpulled me up off the ground and briskly ushered me into the back of the cruiser. I shook in the back seat, trying to make sense of what had just happened. Everything was a haze of blue and white flashes for what seemed forever. Finally, I was able to identify the policeman who arrested me. Of all the cops on the Belltown force, it had to be the one officer who didn't like me—Officer Coughlin. He opened the driver's side door, but didn't get into the car. Instead, he leaned over and grabbed the radio and clicked on to the department, informing them with numbers and letters. I had a strange feeling that I was watching some TV cop show. But I wasn't just watching it—I was in it, and I was starring as the number one suspect. I had to talk some sense into him, but he wouldn't listen to me as he put the radio back on its holder and then slammed the door. Why was he still outside? Why didn't he just drive me to the station? I wondered. After what felt like an eternity, he came back to the cruiser with another officer whom I didn't know. The other officer was carrying something, but I couldn't tell what it was because of the distorted lighting. Officer Coughlin opened the back door. "Are you working with anyone?"

"Working with anyone? What? No! I didn't do this!"

"Of course not. C'mon, I caught you holding the can. Now answer the question!"

"No. I'm not working with anyone, because I didn't do it!" I shouted, frustrated.

Coughlin turned to the other officer. "Bradley, pass me that." The officer passed him the object. "Officer Bradley found this in the woods."

"That's my backpack!" I blurted before I had thought about it.

"Bradley, you heard that. Suspect admits to owning backpack."

"I heard it all right. This will be an easy one."

"If you own the backpack that must mean you own what's inside it." He unzipped the backpack to show me two cans of spray paint, a white sheet, and a book on Hitler.

"Oh, man," I said, defeated. Someone had set me up. "The backpack is mine, but not the other stuff. I can …"

"Save it," Officer Coughlin said and was about to zip it up when he added, "What's this?"

He pulled a green apple out of my backpack. I knew it

wasn't the same one I had brought to the meeting that night because that was lost in the woods somewhere. Also, something about this apple was different. It was fresh looking except for the browning bite mark in the center. I knew what that bite mark meant. The Scarlet Man was laughing. The bite mark meant this was just a little treat for him. What he didn't realize was that I still had some bite left in me!

CHAPTER
NINE

"RABBI SPIELMAN just called. He'll pick you up in ten minutes." Mom frowned while standing in the doorway of our house.

"Oh, thanks." I said softly, as I waited in the driveway.

"Orville, remember you better come home straight after school."

"Yes, Ma'am," I replied as she shut the door. I only used the word "ma'am" whenever Mom was angry, and on this day she was beyond that—she was fuming. Of course, she had every reason to be, and I wasn't the only one she was mad at. Also on the list were Shane and Rabbi Spielman, who confessed to Mom about my involvement in the case. She really let them have it, saying stuff like, "He's just a young boy! These cops and robber games have to stop!" Mom threatened to spill her guts to the Chief, but I pleaded, telling her that Shane would definitely lose his job, so she didn't. Instead, she made Shane promise never to include me in one of his cases again. That hurt, but I told myself for the future to remember that she never mentioned anything about *me* including Shane in one of *my* cases. Also, fortunate for Shane, Officer Coughlin had owed him a huge favor and Shane cashed in. Shane filled Coughlin in and Coughlin then told the chief that he made a mistake arresting me. It had to have been a really big favor for him to do that, I figured. As for Rabbi Spielman, Mom told him that he would have to go to school with me and get back my good name. The Rabbi took half a second to agree. Both Shane and he were feeling so guilty about involving me that she finally forgave them. As for me, that was another story! The most lethal word to a teenager hadn't come from her lips, but it really didn't have to. We both knew it—grounded. That meant missing Vanessa's surprise birthday party tonight, I thought, as I saw Rabbi Spielman's car approaching. It was probably better that way. The guy from the jewelry store had left a message on my machine informing me that he had already sold that perfect gift, and didn't have anything else in my price range. Also, when I called to Gina to tell her about everything and find out if she saw anyone near my coat (she hadn't) she gave me the lowdown on Kip Taylor. His family had just moved to Belltown and he had already become one of the most popular kids at Belltown Academy. All the girls loved him. So my chances with Vanessa were probably zippo. I tried to smile through my depression as I got into Rabbi Spielman's car.

"Tough night last night," he said as we pulled out of the driveway.

"Yeah, and I don't see it getting much better, Rabbi."

"Well, hopefully, Mr. Kapulka's and Gina's idea might help educate the young people in this town."

"What idea?"

"You'll see when we get there."

"Get where, Rabbi?"

"The Belltown Jewish Cemetery."

Students were filing out of the parked rows of school buses and walking into the Belltown Jewish Cemetery when we arrived. "That looks like half the school," I said, as I got out of his car.

"Actually, it's the whole school," the Rabbi answered, and then turned and waved to my principal, Mr. Finn, who was walking toward us.

Mr. Finn shook his hand. "Rabbi, we have a microphone set up so everyone can hear."

Mr. Finn came over to me and shook my hand. "Orville, I knew you were a good kid. Now, if you both will follow me."

"What's going on?" I looked at the Rabbi, but he didn't answer. He just followed Mr. Finn as he kept walking until we came to Nana Goldman's shattered stone. Gina and Mr. Kapulka were standing beside it, and there was a cordless microphone on a stand. I nodded to Gina, and she gave a slight nod, but went back to studying a piece of paper.

"OK, I think we are ready to go," Mr. Finn said into the microphone, and then motioned to the Rabbi to come forward. "If everyone could give us their attention, I would like to introduce you to Rabbi Spielman."

Rabbi Spielman came to the mike. Since we were in a graveyard people didn't know whether to clap or not, so there was a soft patter. I was also confused about what exactly was going on. "Thank you, Mr. Finn. I want to thank you for having the courage to bring your school here this morning. I first want to welcome the students of Belltown High and thank them for their respectful conduct while entering our cemetery. Unfortunately, we are here this morning because not all people have shown that same respect. Before I go any further, I would like to clear up a rumor that you all may have heard about Orville Jacques." The Rabbi waved for me to stand beside him. There were a few whispers, and I was stunned that he was going to tell the whole school.

"Orville said some bad things in his history class about Jewish people. Well, he did that because I had hired him to find out who was committing hate crimes in this town. Orville felt if he went undercover, he would have a better chance to find out who was responsible for these terrible crimes. And he, with the help of Dan Francais, found out some valuable information that the police are now using."

My eyes scanned the crowd for reactions: Franco's big grin, Wayne Rose's shocked glance, and Sue Edward's chilly stare.

"I should add that the police didn't have any knowledge of Orville's work and that is why he was mistakenly arrested last night." I knew that was Rabbi Spielman's way of covering for Shane.

"Are we here because he solved it?" someone asked.

"I only wish that. Unfortunately, we still don't know who did these horrible acts. But we are here for you young people to experience history first hand. Not in the comfort of the classroom, but for you to see that these tombstones are symbols of not just dead people, but living people. People who had to live in conditions we should never forget or we will be doomed to repeat. So, at this time, I humbly give you your classmate, Gina Goldman."

I could see Gina was nervous as she walked to the microphone, but once she began, the nervousness faded, and her purpose drove her on. "Good morning. I want to thank Mr. Kapulka for giving me the opportunity to address you all this morning. This cracked tombstone I am standing next to is my grandmother, Myrna Goldman's stone. I didn't know her as Myrna. I just knew her as Nana. My Nana. I also didn't know her when she was a child, or a young woman with a bright future. I knew her simply as my grandmother, my very loving grandmother. Some of you are lucky to have photo albums filled with pictures of your grandmothers when they were young. I have only one picture." Gina raised the picture to the crowd. "For those of you in the back, I will describe this picture. It is of my grandmother and her twin sister, Esther, when they were three years old. That beautiful woman with them is their mother. This is the only picture I have of my Nana because this was the only one that the Nazis didn't burn in World War II."

There were a few people grumbling, and I think Gina sensed it. "I will get to the point of why I am here. I am here to answer a question that came up in history class this week. Was there a Holocaust?" Gina paused, and I looked over and spotted Sue Edward folding her arms and looking bored. "I would like to read you the letter that was with this picture. On the envelope, it says 'To be opened and read by my grand-daughter, Gina Goldman, when she first faces anti-Semitism.'" Everyone grew silent as Gina cleared her throat. As she read, it was like a voice from the grave had come to life.

Dear Gina,

The fact that you are reading this letter means that the world still harbors hatred over differences. I should start by telling you about the picture with the letter. My twin sister Esther is the other baby in this picture. She was born ten minutes before me but in a way she always seemed years older than I, as will be explained later. If you look closely at the picture, you'll see that my mother is wearing a decorative hairpin. My father gave her that hairpin for her birthday and she loved wearing it. And I guess that is where I should start my story. The last day I saw my mother she was wearing that hairpin. It was three years after this picture was taken. Esther and I were six, and we were barely able to make sense of what was happening. I remember the men in uniforms first dragging my father away from our house and my mother screaming and pleading for them to leave him be. But they didn't. They threw him into a truck, and I never saw him again. Then other uniformed men grabbed Esther, Mother, and me, and I vaguely remember also riding in a truck. But what I remember most was the train. They packed us in, hundreds of women and children in each boxcar. They transported us like herds of animals, but even animals would have had better conditions. It felt like we rode that train for days in the utter darkness without food, water, or fresh air. I wanted to cry, but my eyes were too dry to produce tears. For a while, though, having Mother with Esther and me gave us the strength not to go into shock, like some of the other women and children. She held us tight and her whispered words of love were our only source of comfort as the sounds of death surrounded us. I remember the day the train finally stopped. When they opened the door, the sun I had prayed for blinded me for a while as I tried to focus. Then, I did. They were pushing and pulling us out. And I remember my mother carrying both of us in her arms.

Someone yelled, "Put them down!"

And Mother yelled back, "We will go as a family!"

As we got out of the train, I took a deep breath, expecting to inhale gallons of fresh air, but the air wasn't fresh at all. My nose and throat filled up and choked with the worst odor I have ever smelled. Words on paper could not describe it accurately, but even at age six, I knew it was the odor of death. Esther pointed over to a massive red-brick chimney where black smoke billowed far up into the sky and asked, "Mama, what is that?"

A man in uniform came over and smiled. "That is your new home." I remember my mother putting us down and hitting the man. A second later, he struck her and she fell to the ground. Another soldier rushed over and yelled at the soldier who hit my mother. I remember this soldier was kind to my mother, talking with her softly and pointing at Esther and me. Finally, my mother came over to us and hugged us like she never had or would again. She told us she loved us and I remember her taking off that hairpin and putting it into our little hands, saying, "You have to be big girls now. Go with that man. He promises he'll watch out for you. But hide this hairpin and when you look at it at night, remember you had a loving father who gave it to your mama. And, my little girls, remember you had a mama who loved you. Know that you are loved."

My mother started walking away from us, and I began to chase her. It was the first time during the whole ordeal that she cried, yelling at me, "Go back to your sister, Myrna! Be strong! Be strong!"

Esther, who must have been ahead of her years yelled at me, "Come back, Myrna! Let Mama go! Be strong for Mama!" So, I took one last look at my mother as the line she stood in slowly moved towards the massive chimney, and I went back to Esther. The soldier smiled and took each of our hands and told us everything would be all right. He brought us to a building that seemed different from the others, because it was just for twins like Esther and myself. When we entered the building, the soldier's smile twisted and he roughly snatched the hairpin out of Esther's hands. Before we could do anything, there were people in doctor clothes all around us. Later, a man gave us candy and showed us our room, which was filled with toys. It seemed like we lived there for a long time, but it wasn't that bad, because the man whom we called Uncle Pepi would often bring us sweets like chocolate. He said we were special. The day came when we found out why we were special. A group of doctors brought us into a room and Uncle Pepi was standing there wearing a doctor's mask. Esther told me to run, but before I could, they had me strapped to a slab of marble. I remember seeing Esther and her tiny fists punching Uncle Pepi's waist. Then all I remember is a blinding, sharp white-colored pain. When I woke up my sister Esther was gone, and so was my right arm. Being a twin, I didn't ask if Esther was dead. I knew she was. I felt in my heart that sense of loss, that emptiness. It was years later that I found out that Uncle Pepi amputated my arm without giving me anesthesia. I also found out that Esther and I were only saved from the gas chambers and brick ovens of Auschwitz because we were twins. Uncle Pepi to us was known to the world as Dr. Mengele, the man who conducted the twin experiments in quest for a link to create the perfect race. The world also gave him a nickname—the Angel of Death.

With this knowledge I had to go on and live life. I didn't want Dr. Mengele to win. I couldn't let him win. I vowed on my memories: my father being taken away before I got to know him, my mother's hairpin, and those tiny fists of Esther's, tiny fists that would never give up. I vowed to live a productive life, and I have. I have had a wonderful family, a husband and son. But, there was only one time I regretted having lost my arm. It was the day you were born, my only granddaughter. I could only hold you with one arm. But know this, whenever I have hugged you during your early days in this world, I have hugged you with the power of both arms. And you may be hurting reading this letter, but know that you are loved, my dear. Know that you are loved and be strong. Be strong for Nana and all the other Nanas and Papas who suffered. Be strong.

There were scattered sobs in the crowd of students. Everyone was silent for a long time. Gina stared out into the crowd. There was a teardrop rolling down the side of her cheek, and she said, trying to fight her cracking voice, "To answer that question, Was there a Holocaust?" She paused. "Yes."

I think everyone's eyes bulged as a figure stepped forward. Her face was of stone and no one knew what she was going to do as she walked up to Gina. She looked into Gina's eyes and suddenly Sue Edward reached out and hugged Gina and broke down, saying over and over again, "I am so sorry. I never knew. I never knew. I never knew."

Gina hugged her back. "It's OK. It's OK. It's OK. I forgive you. My Nana forgives you."

I tried to relax on my bed as I read my English book and caught up on some homework. Considering I was grounded, I knew I had plenty of time to get my grades up, and I figured I might as well get right to it. But, as always, my problem was trying to stay focused on my homework assignment. I just couldn't do it. The scene in the graveyard had stayed with me. What Gina had told me about Sue Edward also stuck in my head. After school, they had met at Coffee O to talk. Sue told Gina how Sue's parents raised her the same way they had been raised. Sue was embarrassed and bitter about the way she was brought up and promised that the family tree of hate would stop growing. Gina told me, at that point, she expressed to Sue that it could begin to end if Sue admitted her involvement with the Sons of Hitler and identify their leader. Sue swore to Gina that she had no knowledge of the group, and had nothing to do with the phone calls. I say phone calls, because Shane told me that a phone tip by a young-sounding female is what lead Officer Coughlin to investigate behind the high school, where he found me. Anyway, Gina decided to believe Sue. I wish it had been that easy for me. I felt Sue may have regretted her actions, but probably didn't have enough strength to face the consequences. Sue Edward did have a track record of being an unlikable person, and as much as my forgiving personality wanted to believe her, my detective personality told me something else. It told me, until I got some concrete proof one way or another, Sue Edward was still a suspect. The idea I had earlier to find that proof popped back into my head. I had to call Shane, but just as I was about to get up, there was a knock on The Shack door. I figured it was Mom telling me to come in for dinner, so I stayed on my bed.

"Come in." I thought if Mom saw me on my bed depressed, she might reconsider and let me go to Vanessa's party. It was worth a shot.

"Orville, hurry up. We gotta get going." It was Gina and she was all smiles.

"What are you talking about?"

"Vanessa's party."

"Gina, that's cold. Don't rub it in. You know I'm grounded."

"Beginning tomorrow. I talked with your mom. She's going to let you go."

I jumped up. "You're kidding, right?"

"No, I'm dead serious. We gotta go now, though. We're part of the set-up team. We have to stall Vanessa for about an hour at the hockey game."

" I can't believe Mom changed her mind. What did you say to her?"

"The truth. I told her how you liked Vanessa and this new guy Kip Taylor and she were becoming good friends. I talked to her girl to girl. You know what I mean."

"I can't believe you told my mom all that." I was a little embarrassed because I never really talked to Mom about that kind of stuff.

"Orville, your mom's cooler than you think. Anyway, I also told her if you were stuck here all night you'd probably start thinking about the hate crimes case."

You hit the nail on the head, I thought.

"Your mom said, 'Well, maybe this will at least get his mind off investigating cases and for one night he'll act like the normal teenager I once knew.'"

I smiled because I was really willing to do just that, but I would later learn that fate had another plan.

CHAPTER TEN

"Vanessa's official birthday isn't until tomorrow so she really shouldn't have a clue about the surprise party. So, here's the game plan. Since you were grounded, I had to do the job that her dad intended for you," Gina said as she shifted the gears of her truck.

"What was that?" I asked, glad that Mr. Hyde would have included me in his plans.

"I called her up and asked her if she wanted to go to the hockey game. She told me she was already going. And before you take a fit, Orville, get ready for the bad part. She told me she was going with Kip Taylor. She wanted to introduce him to some of her Belltown High friends."

"Man, this Taylor guy came out of left field," I grunted.

"I know," Gina patted my hand sympathetically. "Anyway, I phoned Kipper . . ."

"Kipper?" I looked at her.

"Well, that's what his mom said:'Kipper, you have a female caller.'" Gina did a snobby impersonation and I had to
laugh. "Anyway," she continued, "I told Kipper the deal. The
really bad news is Kipper has his license and his own BMW,
which he was only too happy to tell me. He's planning to
drive Vanessa to the game, and meet us there. The game starts
at six-thirty. At seven-thirty Dan and I will tell Vanessa that we
have to drive you home because you're still in trouble for the
other night."

I tried to ignore the Kip Taylor info and focus on something lighter. I smiled because I knew Gina was trying to slip
something by me. "Did I hear you say Dan? As in Franco?"

"You know that's what you heard. He's coming to the
party as my date. We're meeting him at the game."

"So, that is what the big hurry was all about. I mean,
look, we still have a good half hour before the game." I pointed
at the clock under the dashboard.

"Well, I have to admit I'm a little nervous, and I must
have misread the clock in my house before I came for you."

"Man, Gina, I could have taken a quick shower and
changed my clothes. I look like a grub. That Kip Taylor guy
will show up all stylin' in his BMW ...." I paused in frustration
for a second. "I can't believe he has his own car. It's bad enough
he has a license. I mean, I have to wait another three weeks
before I can even get a chance to finish my student driving,
never mind going for my license. By then, they'll probably
have gone on a thousand dates in his fancy car. Wait a second ..."

"What?" Gina asked.

"Gina, do you know Miss Turner, the Driver's Ed. teacher?"

"Yeah, she taught me to drive. Why?"

"Because she has an apartment right by the ice arena," I said, thinking impulsively.

"Yeah, I know where she lives. Why?"

"I have to talk to her tonight and beg her to let me finish up my driving next week. It's not like we don't have plenty of time. Let's face it, you don't want to show up early to meet Franco. You were going to make him sweat, remember?" I teased her.

"Actually, I think we can spare ten minutes." Gina looked at me. "Maybe Miss Turner will let you use her bathroom so you can freshen up for Vanessa. You have some serious bedhead." She pointed and giggled.

"What?" I looked into her rear-view mirror and noticed she wasn't joking. My hair was all over the place. It looked like I put my finger in a light socket.

"Gina, step on it. It's an emergency!"

Gina laughed, pumping the gas pedal once to continue the joke, and then spun the wheel and headed for Miss Turner's street.

"She must not be home," Gina concluded after she rang the doorbell for the third time.

"But her lights are on and her car …" I began, but was interrupted by Miss Turner's voice on the other side of the door, "Come on in, it's open."

Gina opened the door, and I followed her as she walked into Miss Turner's apartment. From the outside, the apartment was modest looking at best, so I wasn't expecting much inside. Boy, was I wrong. I don't know much about decorating, but standing in Miss Turner's living room, I knew the woman had taste.

"Wow, who's her interior decorator?" Gina whispered, as Miss Turner came through the door saying, "I thought we agreed you'd ..." She stopped when she saw us. She looked a little shaken. "Oh, Orville and Gina. Oh, I ... I am sorry, I was expecting my neighbor. She wanted to borrow some eggs. You caught me off guard." She put her arms out to show her appearance. She was wearing a cooking apron.

"Well, that's good to know. It's not safe to just let anyone walk in." I gave an uneasy smile. I got the feeling I probably made a mistake by invading Miss Turner's privacy.

"Yes, well, what can I do for you two?"

Before I could answer Gina said, "Miss Turner, have you been crying?"

"Oh, this." Miss turner wiped her eyes dry and pointed her thumb behind her, "I was just ... Well, actually, yes Gina. I was just listening to the radio making a little dinner and heard about today in the cemetery. The reporter talked about how you read from your grandmother's letter to the school. It is ironic that you dropped by. I'm so sorry for you, Gina, but you really showed a lot of courage."

Gina shrugged. "Thanks. I didn't think Mr. Finn was going to tell the media."

"He probably didn't. You know reporters, though. Now, what can I do for you two?" Miss Turner wiped her eyes again.

Now I really felt like a jerk. Compared to everything else, my driving privileges didn't seem important.

"Miss Turner, we probably shouldn't have stopped by. But we were driving by and well ... You know how I was able to talk to you about that girl Vanessa I like?"

Miss Turner gave me the "go on" look.

"Well, there is this new guy in town. I think he likes her and he has his own car and license. And well, I was wondering about my driving ..."

"Oh, that's all. Oh, I get it. This is about the note I put into your homeroom folder. I just wanted you to think before the next time you miss one of your driving days. We will resume your schedule next week. I understand you want to get your license so you can take the girl out." Miss Turner smiled for the first time, and I lost my breath for a moment. "Thanks, Miss Turner. You're the best. You really understand us kids."

"No problem, Orville. Well, I'd better get back ..."

"One other thing. Can I use your bathroom for a minute?" I pointed to my flyaway hair.

She hesitated, but then smiled. "Sure. Go through there and it's the second door on the left." She pointed, and as I went through the door I heard her ask Gina, "What are you guys up to tonight?"

In the bathroom, I wet down my hair and ran my comb through it. I gave a look in the mirror and, although I didn't look like the next GQ coverboy, I was satisfied I at least looked presentable. I was heading back towards her living room when I heard the teakettle screaming in the kitchen. "I'll get it!" I hollered and rushed into the kitchen and turned it off. At that point, I felt like a complete jerk when I noticed the table was set for two, including wine glasses and an unlit candle in the center. I spotted cut mushrooms, green and red peppers, and half an onion resting on the chopping block. I had barged in and interrupted Miss Turner while she had been preparing a romantic dinner. Feeling like an idiot, I hurried back to the living room and said, "Miss Turner, I'm sorry we've bothered you. We'll get going now."

Miss Turner remained pleasant, but she did usher us to the door. "It's OK, Orville. I understand. By the way, I'm sorry Grant couldn't help you out with the gift for Vanessa. But his father didn't want to …"

"Oh no!" I blurted and realized I interrupted Miss Turner. "I'm sorry, Miss Turner. But I still don't have a gift for Vanessa."

"That's right." Gina realized. "If we hurry, you can buy her a CD or something."

"Yeah, thanks again, Miss Turner." We hustled out her door.

Miss Turner stood in the doorway. "You could also promise her a romantic night out when you get your license."

We waved goodbye and I thought, if that were to happen, then whose birthday would it be?

Fortunately, I didn't have to skim through too many CDs because I remembered Vanessa once told me she loved the music from the movie *Braveheart*. In fact, she had told me that she would love to use that music in one of her figure skating programs sometime. So when I spotted the CD I snatched it up and paid the cashier. I knew it wasn't the "perfect gift" to show how I felt, but it was pretty thoughtful for a rush job. When we got to the game, it took only seconds for me to spot Vanessa's long blond hair in the crowd of spectators. She was talking to a group of girls, introducing Kip Taylor. Kip was smiling and shaking hands and his eyes caught mine.

"Hey, Vanessa. It's your friend Orville." I may have been reading into it, but it sounded like he stressed the word "friend."

"Orville, what's up? I thought you were in trouble with your mom because of last night. Gina told me everything about how you were set up." Vanessa was talking a mile a minute.

"Yeah, I can only stay here for an hour or so."

"Ah, that's too bad. I thought all of us could go out after the game." She at least seemed genuinely disappointed.

"Oh, Orville. Can you excuse me for a second? I see my figure skating coach, and I have to ask her about my practice schedule. You can keep Kip company." Vanessa took off into the crowd leaving me alone with the Kipper. I looked around for Gina for help, but she was by the soda machine talking in depth to Franco.

"So, Orville. I didn't really get to talk to you last night, since you got busted and all." Kip laughed.

"Yeah." I tried to ignore him.

"Vanessa tells me that you try to solve mysteries. What's *that* all about?" he asked, talking down to me. I felt my temperature rising, but I answered coolly, "I try to help people when they need it."

He laughed. "Like the young Sherlock Holmes, or the young Indiana Jones. Or maybe like the Hardy boys or more like Encyclopedia Brown. You got the glasses for that." He laughed some more.

"Or maybe just like the young Orville Jacques," I said coldly, and he caught it.

"Hey, I'm just kidding around," Kip said, and then faked interest. "Do you ever get lucky and solve any?"

"Why don't you ask Vanessa's dad that question. If you'd excuse me for a second, Kipper." When I saw the pained expression on his face, I bit the side of my mouth and walked away. Like the name Orville, Kip obviously hadn't chosen his name and by his face, he certainly hadn't chosen his nickname. It was a juvenile jab on my part, but I really didn't care. In a few moments of talking with him, I didn't see a friendship forming between Kip Taylor and me.

"Orville, can I talk with you for a second?" Wayne Rose had a guilty look on his face.

"Sure, Wayne. What can I do for you?"

"I think you know what it's about. I just want to apologize …"

"Stop right there, Wayne. You don't have to apologize at all. How were you to know I was working undercover?"

"I know, but you're a friend of mine. I should have thought more about your character before I blew up on you." Wayne shook his head.

"You know that's crazy talk. I'm just glad most of the school did react to my comments. The scary thing would have been if no one said anything."

"Yeah, no matter what has happened, we do have a good school," he agreed.

"By the way, I thought you showed a lot of courage last night at the town rally. You'd make a great class president, Wayne."

"I showed courage?" he laughed. "Anyone can give a speech. Not everyone can fight for the greater good without any regard to his own person reputation. Orville, you did that."

"I really never thought of it that way," I said.

"That's my point, my friend." He shook my hand and this time, hearing the word friend stressed brought a good feeling, a really good feeling.

It was that good feeling circulating through my body that made me unable to fight the urge I got when I saw there was no line at the payphone. Usually at the hockey games, the line at the payphones was endless. "One quick phone call," I said to myself, and pumped in some coins and pegged Shane's digits.

Shane picked up after one ring. "Detective O'Connell."

"Shane, it's me, Orville."

"Oh, man, Orville. I don't think it's a good idea to talk to you. Your mom could have my job."

"She doesn't have enough training," I joked.

"That's not funny. You know what I mean." Shane was serious.

"OK, I'll make it quick. I was thinking about the first 911 call dispatch received about the cemetery."

"What about it?"

"Doesn't the address of a phone call come up on the dispatch operator's computer screen?"

"Yes," Shane agreed.

"So, I figure the 911 operator may have been listening to the caller telling the address but didn't check the screen to see if the call was coming from a different address. So, if you just check the address that was on the screen, you'll know where your caller was. Like if they were in their own house or at a convenience store," I said, having a vision of Sue Edward in her room at three o'clock in the morning making the call. "I mean, it must be on the computer files or something," I added.

"Orville, I have to admit, you are good."

"Thanks," I smiled into the receiver.

"But you're not giving our 911 operator enough credit. She was also focused on the screen that night."

"I don't get it. Why wouldn't the address come up?" I asked, thinking that it always did whenever I watched the show "911."

"The caller explained to the operator that she was using a cell phone. Our system can't trace cell phones. We have to go by their word, and why would we question that? And even if we could trace them, I wouldn't be surprised if she made the call from a cell phone in the vicinity of the cemetery. Probably the same thing happened with the phone tip about you."

"Ah, man!" I said in disgust.

"How do you think I feel? I have all of that going on, not to mention another house was broken into last night. I actually thought that you were Eve Capshaw. I promised her an interview about how the crime rate has risen in Belltown in the last two years. She's really going to grill me with questions when I tell her that we almost caught the robber driving away from the scene, but they lost two of our cruisers on the backroads."

"What kind of car were they driving?"

"Can you believe they were going so fast our guys couldn't positively ID it? Anyway, Miss Capshaw has caught onto my theory that it all could be connected to the hate crimes." He laughed for a minute. "But how am I going to connect a boot with white paint on the heel with a red fingernail? Man, it sounds like a game of Clue."

"Wait. What did you say about a red fingernail?"

"Oh, that's right. I didn't tell you about that. In the house that was robbed we found a red fingernail."

I felt a tug on my coat as an annoyed girl said, "Hurry up."

"OK, one second," I said to her. "Go on, Shane."

"That's it, Orville. Anyway, I gotta get going. That's my call waiting. See ya, Orville." Shane hung up and the first thing I thought of was when Sue Edward was putting on red press-on nails in history class.

"It took you long enough," the girl said as she went over to the phone.

"Yeah, you can say that again," I said to myself, and headed for Franco and Gina.

I told Gina and Franco about my phone call to Shane and how I had seen Sue Edward putting on the red press-on nails in class.

"It can't be Sue. It just can't. She gave me her word that she had nothing to do with it," Gina said, looking as though she had just been punched in the stomach.

"I'm sorry, Gina," I said.

"Some people just can't change." Franco put his arm around her shoulder.

"But in the cemetery she seemed so genuine. And when I talked with her today, she didn't waiver when she looked me in the eye and said she wasn't involved."

Franco and I didn't know what to say. But then a strange smile came across Gina's face. "Wait! Orville, you and Franco missed it."

"Missed what?" we asked.

"If anything, this evidence clears Sue Edward of any wrongdoing. Shane told you that they found a red fingernail. Not a *fake* fingernail."

"I know, but I figure that's why she was putting on the fake nails in the first place—because she broke one when breaking into the house last night."

"Do you hear yourself?" Gina smiled.

"Last night. That's right. I saw Sue putting on the fake nails the other day in class. She couldn't have broken a real one last night." I couldn't believe I missed the obvious again.

"Plus, Sue bites her nails to the quick. From her upbringing, I can see why," Gina added. "Anyway, a fingernail has to be at least long enough to break." She stopped for a second and again thought to herself and said, "No, that's crazy. No way. It couldn't be. Yeah … crazy."

"What's crazy?" Franco and I urged.

"You're going to laugh me right out of here, but … Well,

tonight when we were at Miss Turner's and Orville went into the bathroom, I noticed she had a Band-Aid on her forefinger. She said she had a bad day and that she even broke a nail, so she was going to snuggle up with a good book and call it a night. It's just a coincidence," Gina surmised.

Franco laughed. "Miss Turner. Gina, that's a good one."

But I didn't laugh, because Gina's statement hit me hard. "Miss Turner didn't tell you she was having someone over for dinner?"

"No, Orville. Why?"

"Oh, man!" I couldn't believe it, but the wave of answers suddenly showered me at once and I didn't know where to begin except to say, "She's with them."

"With who?" they both asked.

"The Sons of Hitler."

"What, are you crazy?" Franco said.

"I said it was just a coincidence. Miss Turner is a nice woman. You saw her crying tonight about what happened at the cemetery," Gina said. But my mind was telling me something Shane had said about always listening with your eyes, your head, and your gut, because that's what's really talking. My gut was talking loud and clear.

"I saw her crying, but it wasn't about that. Gina, Miss Turner told you that she wasn't having company, but I saw her table set for two."

"Yeah, well she probably didn't want us blabbing it around the school that she had a date."

"True, but she explained that she had tears in her eyes because of what she heard on the radio about you at the cemetery. When I went into her kitchen, I didn't hear the radio playing."

"So, she turned it off," Gina said.

"Wait," Franco interrupted. "I listened to the radio on the way here with my dad and there was no mention of Gina and what happened today."

"Well, she probably has a good ex…"

"Gina, let me finish, and then you can stand up for her. The answers are flying at me. I have to get them out. You asked why she was crying. In the kitchen I saw a bunch of vegetables. All of them were cut up on a chopping block, except for half an onion. She hadn't finished cutting the onion, because Gina and I interrupted her. That's why she came to the door with tears in her eyes. She had tears in her eyes because she had been cutting an onion. Not because of Gina at the cemetery."

"What?" they said in amazement, and then, "Go on, Orville."

"With that fingernail, that makes it pretty suspicious. But let's look at other things. Her apartment. Franco, you should have seen the inside of this place. How could she decorate it on a teacher's salary, Gina?"

Gina nodded. "He's right. Inside is beautiful."

"Also, Shane said crimes have gone up in Belltown in the last two years. Miss Turner has only been here for two years. Also, Shane couldn't believe how this person kept getting away. Well, Franco, you heard Miss Turner tell us that being a Driver's Ed. teacher she knows every road and backroad in town. Plus the fact that she knows about *us*. The students. We trust her. So we tell her things. I remember her asking me if my family was going away to visit my dad in Ireland. She was probably casing the joint." I was excited.

"I can't believe this, but it's not as farfetched as I thought," Franco admitted.

"But, what about the Sons of Hitler? Where do they fit in?" Gina was still on the fence.

"Good question. That's the only thing I don't get. Maybe she works for them recruiting members. All I know is, I think it has something to do with the other place setting at her table," I said, deciding to hold in my other hunch until I had more proof.

At that moment, all three of us felt a presence behind us. We turned around and a look of fear came over the face of the eavesdropper— the quiet equipment manager, Matt Dunn. A second later, he took off into the crowd.

"Orville, look at his boots!" Franco pointed at the white paint spot on the back heel as Matt made a mad dash out of the building. Franco caught up to him in no time and tackled him. A group of teachers and students ran over and crowded around Franco and Matt. Mr. Finn and Mr. Kapulka pulled Franco off and restrained him, giving Matt Dunn enough time to get up and take off out the front door of the arena. Gina and I tried to get through the crowd to help Franco, but a couple of ice arena employees dragged him into the office.

"Gina, we gotta get Miss Turner before Dunn warns her!" I yelled and she nodded. We both sprinted to her truck, and she put it in gear and hauled out of the parking lot headed for Miss Turner's apartment. But we had no idea exactly what we were going to do once we got there.

"It's a fine time for your CB to break," I cursed as I hooked it back on its holder.

"Well, maybe if you waited for me to show you how to use it, it wouldn't have busted!" Gina shot back as we approached Miss Turner's road. We were both jumpy.

Gina tried to get back in control. "Look, I can turn around and go to the gas station up the street. I bet they have a phone. You can call Shane from there."

I tried to follow Gina's lead and said calmly, "It's a good idea, but I'm afraid if Matt Dunn finds a phone, he'll call her before that. So we might as well go to her apartment and hope by now Franco has explained everything. When he sees we're gone, he'll send the cops here."

Gina parked a few houses up the street and then turned to me. "We have two choices: stake out her apartment and wait for the cops, or sneak up and look through her window and spy on her."

"What good would it do to spy on her? I just wanted to be in the position to follow her if she got the call, and her car is right there," I pointed, content on staying put.

"Well, I'm just thinking if Matt Dunn does call, which we're not sure he will, she'll be warned. One, she could arm herself. Two, if she makes it to her car, we're really playing by her rules. I would try to follow her but you know she'd lose us in no time with her driving ability and all the side roads she knows."

"Geez, I never thought of that. You got a plan?" I asked, clueless.

"We sneak up and look through her back window. If she is by herself, we ring her bell and make another excuse to come in. When we get in, we overpower her, lock her in a room, and call 911. But, if she is with the dinner date, we don't do anything except take a good look at him so we can ID him later. Well, what do you think?"

"Well, I can't think of any better plans," I admitted, and reached to open my door, but someone beat me to it.

"I have a different plan," Miss Turner said as she pointed a shiny silver gun at my eyes.

"Oh, my …" I put my hands up.

"Get out of the truck." She looked around and thought again as she spotted another truck coming down the street. "No. Stay in the truck!" She hopped in beside me and dug the gun into my side with one hand and shut the door with the other.

"I can't believe this. It really is true," Gina gasped. Gina had been going along with my hunch, but now having the barrel of a gun pointed at me, the realization had hit her. That was the same feeling I had. After all, I had been wrong on my hunches about Paul Miller and Sue Edward. Part of me had thought that this hunch would also slap me back in the face. That was until Miss Turner waved her silver gun.

"Shut up! Shut up! When that truck parks I want you to beep once. Just once. You hear me, Gina? Twice and you'll both regret it. Better still, don't do that. I want you to flick your beams on and off." It was an eerie feeling as Miss Turner instructed Gina. If she hadn't been pointing a gun at me, I would have thought we were at Driver's Ed. Gina flicked the beams as the man got out of the truck. The truck was close enough that I could make out some of the license plate. It was an Arizona plate that began with the letter P. No wonder

Shane couldn't trace the blue pickup truck, I thought. He was looking it up as a Massachusetts plate. Where did I hear Arizona? I wondered. The man shielded his face from the beams with his hand and Miss Turner ordered, "Flick them off. Now."

Miss Turner then rolled the window down with her free hand and whispered loudly, "It's me, Eleanor. Get over here."

The man hurried over to the passenger door and said, "Eleanor, what are you doing in there?" And then he saw us and said something in a foreign language. By the tone, I guessed he was cursing. It was the same language he used that night on the beach. I stared at the red ruby ring glistening in the moonlight and then stared into the face of the person I had called the Scarlet Man, but this time he wasn't wearing a scarlet sheet. He was wearing anger all over his face. But suddenly, like the tide going out to sea, the anger left him and the face of jewelry store owner Grant D'Leeder now wore the worst expression of all. An expressionless stare with the unfeeling eyes of a shark as he simply said, "You know what this means, Eleanor. This means we have to kill them."

Miss Turner quickly told Grant D'Leeder about Matt Dunn calling to warn her. At this D'Leeder said, "That's the only thing that kid ever did right. We wouldn't be in this if he didn't write that letter inviting Jacques to a meeting, not to mention inviting Francais."

"I know, Grant."

"Eleanor, let's not forget how you tried to recruit Jacques also by bringing him by the store."

"I know, Grant. I shouldn't have gone by what he said in his class. I should have known better. But what are we going to do?"

"We'll figure it out at the store." He jumped into his truck and started it up.

"Follow him," was all Miss Turner said, and we were quiet for a minute. Then Gina looked over from behind the steering wheel. "Why, Miss Turner? You don't strike me as the racist type."

"I'm not. For me it isn't about that. It's about love and money. Grant promises me lots of money when we get married. You see, our relationship began out of convenience. He was conducting a meeting one night in the clearing when he caught me driving down that unused dirt road. I promised him I wouldn't tell anyone."

"And he trusted you? Why didn't he just ... y'know," I didn't want to use the word so she did. "Why didn't he kill me? He was going to until he found out I was using that road because I had just robbed a house. That night he fell in love with my devious mind," she cracked a smile.

"You mean you were robbing houses before the Sons of Hitler?" Gina asked in shock.

"Yes, ever since I was a teenager. And in this town, it was so easy. I had the perfect cover. Who would suspect a Driver's Ed. teacher? Anyway, I fell in love with Grant and he's going to give me what my family couldn't and wouldn't give. In a few weeks we'll be far away from ..." she realized she was talking too much .

"Can I ask you how Matt Dunn got involved?" I wondered if Miss Turner would bite. She did. I think she felt if she talked, she wouldn't be nervous. She may have been crazy and robbed houses, but it looked to me like she had never used a gun.

"Grant came from Arizona because his father had to go into a nursing home. He's going to sell the store. Anyway, he wanted to start a Sons of Hitler chapter in Belltown. He had a couple of members, but he wanted younger boys. So, I just talked to kids in Driver's Ed. and found out about them. Matt was lonely. He doesn't have a father, and so when I introduced him to Grant, he was a natural candidate. Grant has taught Matt the ways of the group. Matt has made some mistakes, but he did talk the hockey team into shaving their heads so Matt could become a skinhead and not be noticed. Anyway, it's Grant's mission to find the Matt Dunns of the world to spread the words of Hitler."

"You're absolutely crazy!" Gina couldn't hold it in, and Miss Turner yelled, "Shut up! No more! I want it quiet until we get there, or you'll see just how crazy I am." She waved the gun menacingly. For the next ten minutes, we didn't dare say a word. I knew it was no idle threat. She meant business.

"Go in there, now!" D'Leeder, who was now also carrying a gun, pointed with it to the back room of the jewelry store. When Gina and I walked in, the door slammed behind us. I scanned for possible exits or anything we could use to defend ourselves—nothing. It was a storage room with nothing but a bunch of boxes.

"Orville, what are we going to do?" Gina was white with fear.

"I don't know. Let's listen. Maybe we can get a plan if we can hear what *they're* planning." I pressed my ear against the door. I could hear D'Leeder talking.

"We'll take them with us to New Hampshire. Have it done there. That way, if anything bad happens, we can use them as hostages. If not, there are a lot of woods up there. Some archeologist will find them a hundred years from now. I'll do it quick." He made a popping noise.

"Even if they're dead, we still can't come back here. Matt or the other members will talk." Miss Turner sounded nervous.

"Eleanor, trust me. Don't be nervous, everything will be all right. I know we can't come back here. In a week, we'll be skiing in the Alps." I heard the sound of a kiss followed by, "I can't call my people from here in case the cops check the phone records. Do you have that cell phone?"

Miss Turner replied, "It's in my car, parked in the garage in the back. I'm sorry. I'll go get it."

"That's OK, Eleanor. I'll call when we're on the road. That's one of the reasons we came here. More trunk space for them. And, Eleanor, you know the other reason why we came here."

I didn't hear her respond. All I heard is what I guessed was the jewelry trays being cleaned out and dumped into a container. Then is was quiet for a minute and Gina and I gave each other looks wondering if they had left. Of course, it was desperate thinking on our part, because then the door burst open and D'Leeder was carrying something while Miss Turner kept her gun on us.

"Here, carry this and walk in front of me."

I almost froze when I realized what it was—the same gray metal trunk from the Belltown Hospital Thrift Store.

"Oh my God. You murdered Clark Harrison," I said in shock.

"How did you know that?" D'Leeder was also shocked.

"The gray trunk. I was there when he bought it. I can't believe... why?"

"Any chance you had to live you just blew with your big mouth," D'Leeder snarled.

"I know you're going to kill us, so at least show the respect of giving me an explanation. Why did you kill Clark Harrison over a worthless trunk?"

"Worthless if you didn't open it or look at the markings on the bottom of it. Fortunately for my family, Harrison was the only one who did. On the bottom of the trunk is a swastika."

A quick flash came to me talking with Scotty Donovan and his saying, "There was something ... and now it's pretty strange..." Scotty had seen the swastika.

"What's in the trunk?" Gina asked.

D'Leeder took a long look at her and then smiled. "We really don't have time, but in view of who I am talking with I will make some. I know father would want it that way."

"Grant, we really ..." Miss Turner began and D'Leeder snapped at her in a foreign tongue.

"That is German for shut up—the language of the Fatherland. When I was young my father taught me to speak our language and he taught me the old ways. The right ways. You see, our real name is Schmidt. My father changed it when he was fleeing Germany. They wanted to charge him for war crimes. He had a wonderful sense of humor by changing our name to D'Leeder and naming his only son Grant. Grant D'Leeder," he laughed for a minute. "When this metal trunk first came to America with my father it was filled with jewelry that he had confiscated from Jews when they came into the camps. In the early days of this shop, he sold that jewelry to get the store on its feet. But then he stopped in fear that it might be traced. But now and again he would put a piece out on the display table and sell it. He said he got a certain satisfaction doing that. It made him feel like he was still part of the war."

I looked over at Gina and I thought she was going to try to strangle D'Leeder. My eyes pleaded with her to remain cool, but even I couldn't handle what I was about to hear.

He pointed to Gina. "Of course, my father stopped putting out any of the remaining pieces after your grandmother came in and recognized a hairpin."

"What!" we yelled.

"She went into shock when she saw that hairpin and then recognized my father as the same soldier who worked with Dr. Mengele."

"What! You're lying!" Gina cried.

"I thought you'd say that." D'Leeder pulled the hairpin out of his coat pocket and threw it at Gina's feet.

"It can't be! It can't be!" Gina sobbed as she reached down for the pin.

"Yes, your grandmother died from a stroke in this store. A stroke of good luck for my father, wouldn't you say?" He smiled.

"Why you ..." My anger almost overtook my thinking as I began to charge, but both guns forced me back.

"Get back! You can live a few more hours or I can end it right now!"

"You'll never get away. They'll catch you," I said, not really believing it myself.

"See this ring? This is our ticket out of here. Hitler gave rings to his special people. My father was one of them. Hitler liked my father, and so did Dr. Mengele. Dr. Mengele even kept in touch with my father over the years, sending him letters from South America. Dr. Mengele's friends even set up many Swiss bank accounts for people like my father. Of course, it was money they took from the Jews. I will use some of that money to give Eleanor a good life, and the rest to fund a new organization. My father etched those account numbers into the bottom of this trunk. So you see, I had no intention of staying here in Belltown. I just wanted to get a few of the young people thinking about the power of Hitler. So, we *are* going to get away. Now, let's go."

"One more question." Stall, stall, stall, I thought.

"One more, Jacques, and that's it."

"If the trunk is so important, then how did it end up donated at the thrift store?"

"That imbecile, Matt Dunn. Since I put my father in a nursing home, I put a number of items in another box and told Matt to get rid of it. He picked the wrong box and then he had his mother drive him to the thrift store to drop it off. Now, let's go!"

When we got to the garage in the back of the store, D'Leeder forced Gina and me to squeeze into the trunk of a black Town Car. "I'll see you in New Hampshire," he said as he slammed the trunk door on us, shutting us into a world of darkness. Part of me wanted to let the fear invade my body and take over, but I fought it. I had to. I had to remain calm. It was our only chance for survival. I had been in situations like this before, and I knew staying focused on escaping would be our best chance. I needed Gina to be on that same page, but she was gasping uncontrollably. "Gina, you have to stop that! I need you!"

"My Nana. I can't believe this. Any of this. They killed her." She was going into shock. I knew she was right. He may not have pulled a trigger, but Schmidt did kill Nana Goldman. I was losing Gina and I had to say something fast.

"You're right, Gina. He did kill your Nana. And from what we know he's still alive. Do you want his son to kill you and have him win? We're going to get out of this and the Schmidts are going to spend the rest of their lives in prison. But I need you to be strong. Remember Nana's letter!"

My words worked. Gina instantly snapped out of it, just as the car began rolling down onto the road. "OK, you're right, Orville. I'm sorry. What's the plan?" she asked above the humming of the car and road.

"Good that's better." I have her back, I thought, now I need a plan. "The only good thing is we have about three hours or so to think of a plan." I tried to be optimistic, thinking that our next stop was New Hampshire. "Feel around on your side for any crow bars or anything we can use for a weapon," I suggested, as my hands wandered in search of something. We didn't talk for a minute as our search proved futile.

"He must have cleaned everything out before," I said and then the car took a sharp right and my head slammed against some hard padding, while one of my fingers got stuck in a hole of some sort. "Owwww."

"Are you OK, Orville?"

"Yeah, I just banged my head and I think I cut my finger. It's stuck in a hole by the taillight." I counted to three to myself and tugged it out. I couldn't see it, but I felt blood trickle. At that moment, I remembered something I had seen on TV. It was on one of those television news magazine shows. At the time, I laughed thinking who would ever need this knowledge. Now, I realized how valuable it was.

"Gina, pull up the padding next to you," I said, as I ripped at the padding next to me. It was easier than I thought as the section opened up. I wormed my hand down and felt wires going in different directions. I squinted one eye down and could see a little light. The wires were connected to the taillight. I started to tremble with excitement, but I didn't say anything.

"I did it, Orville. I feel a bunch of wires. Now what?"

"I don't think we'll get a shock, but it's better than the alternative. Just tug at them and maybe we can disconnect the taillights."

"Oh yeah! I get what you mean!" It registered and now Gina was also getting excited. If I didn't have such an adrenaline rush I may have felt the zap that singed my fingers for a moment. I squinted down through the hole and there was no sign of light. "My side is out," I said and Gina let out an "Owww! I think mine is out, too."

For the next few minutes we were back to being powerless, and my mind was beginning to shift back into the negative state. What if we make it all the way to New Hampshire without any taillights? I knew what that "what if" would lead to. But, just when the negativity was clouding my hope, a distant siren sounded and grew louder and louder and louder, and D'Leeder's car began too go slower and slower and slower, until we came to a stop and his engine turned off. I heard a car door shut, the sound of footsteps and then bits and pieces of words. "What seems ... Officer?"

"Taillights ... out ..."

"Orville, it's a cop. It worked." Gina began to bang.

"No, Gina!" I snapped and the force of my voice made her stop instantly.

"What do you mean, no?"

"Wail till you hear the officer walk by here again. If we yell now, he'll be ambushed." I had a picture of the officer standing at the driver's door and turning his head at the sound of our banging and yelling, giving D'Leeder just enough time to pull his gun and have an easy shot. It was bad enough that the officer would have to be ready to react, but I figured clearing the driver's side would give him enough distance to pull his gun and have a fair chance. I only hoped that they thought we couldn't hear at all under the heavy trunk. And we really couldn't—just fragments of conversation.

"You have that fixed in the morning ... folks have a good night ..."

We could barely make out the sound of the footsteps, but they were passing as we banged and screamed, "They have guns! Watch out!"

"Put it down!" I think the officer yelled, but then a gunshot rang out followed by a volley. There was nothing we could do but listen, and my stomach turned as the car went into motion. Our bodies slid back and forth as our heads bumped into each other while the car made screeching turns. A wailing siren echoed, and then more and more joined the chorus of noise as the car zigzagged from side to side. Gina and I held onto one another, praying that this carnival ride would end. But, we had no way of knowing by the sounds and hard turns. Then suddenly, I didn't hear the sounds of the road below. I had the strange sense that we were floating in air, but that feeling ended just as quickly as we slammed into something and came to a stop.

I heard yelling, "Get them out!"

"We're in here!" We both banged and then I felt the car sinking forward. I couldn't figure it out until I heard a gushing sound and felt cold water seeping through the trunk.

"Oh, no!" we yelled, as the water was quickly filling up the trunk. "Help! Help!"

There was a banging sound on the trunk and the metal was dangerously denting closer to us. I didn't know what would get us first—the water or the piercing metal. But then the trunk popped open and there, standing, wielding a sledgehammer, was my good friend and mentor, Shane O'Connell. Two officers pulled us out of the car. I looked around and couldn't believe our luck. The car had flown off the Belltown dock and crashed into a forty-foot sailboat. It was slowly sinking with the boat. In a few minutes, they would both be at the bottom. I shivered at the thought that if we hadn't hit that boat, we would have gone straight down, and that would have put us in a position from which only Houdini would have been able to escape.

After a few seconds, I was able to talk. "Shane, are they dead?"

"Nope. Cuffed and stuffed." He pointed over at the cruiser.

"Man, I owe you my life."

"I'll just put it on your tab," he smiled, and ruffled my wet hair.

I won't even get into how angry Mom was when she heard what had happened, but for some reason she let me go to the courthouse the next day. There was a busload of people from the Sons of Hitler who were going to be arraigned and one of them was Matt Dunn, who was caught moments after his phone tip to Miss Turner. Matt Dunn had confessed to recruiting members as young as the fourth grade, but he denied any knowledge of D'Leeder murdering Clark Harrison. Dunn ID'd every member in the Belltown chapter, hoping for a lighter sentence, but what he received was far different from what anyone imagined—but I'll get to that in a minute. First item: full name, Guenter Schmidt. I didn't go with Gina and Shane when they went to the Shady Lane Nursing Home. I felt that should be Gina's time to confront the evil that haunted her family's past. I asked Gina if she said anything to Guenter Schmidt before they took him away. And she only said, "I told him I was sorry for him, and I forgave him for what he did."

I couldn't believe it. "How could you forgive him?"

Gina ignored my outrage, looked down at the hairpin in her hand, and said with a smile, "I think I'm going to grow my hair long. Real long."

I smiled back, but I still couldn't understand why she forgave the man responsible for so much pain, suffering, and death. I didn't know it, but I was going to learn the lesson Gina was trying to teach.

Matt Dunn's mother stood in the courtroom crying, "I can't afford bail. I work two jobs as it is. He's just a boy."

Judge McCarthy, the toughest judge in the county, said, "Ma'am, I'm sorry for you. But spray painting one swastika might be considered a minor offense, but we're not talking about just one. What he has done is far beyond that. And in my court, you don't get just a slap on the wrist. I'm sorry."

Mrs. Dunn turned to Matt. "Why? Why did you do this? I work so hard to pay your medical bills and give you a good life, and this is how you repay me? Why did you do this? Why are you so angry?"

"Because he is afraid," a voice said. It wasn't chastising. It was more of a voice of understanding. It was Jonah Stein. He came forward. "If I may address the court, your Honor?"

"Yes, Mr. Stein. You are one of the victims of this young man's alleged vandalism, are you not?"

"I am, and I would like to post bail for him. And I know he has other charges against him, but I'm willing to drop mine. Under one condition."

Everyone in the courtroom gasped and Judge McCarthy banged his gavel. "Order, order. This is very unusual. May I ask why you are helping this young man not to pay for his crime?"

"Oh, that is not my intention at all. Part of the arrangement would be that Matt Dunn fixes the destruction he caused in my work barn."

Judge McCarthy said to Matt, "What is your response to that?"

Matt didn't answer until his mother whispered to him. "Yes," he stammered. "But …"

"But what?" the judge asked.

"But why is he doing this?"

Judge McCarthy said, "That's what I'd like to know, Mr. Stein."

"It is not easy for me to forgive, but we have to start or the problem will get worse. And we have to educate the young. I want to educate Mr. Dunn about the pain that fills me every time I see a swastika. We can't erase that pain of our past, but we can teach our children so it won't happen again. I know deep down Matt Dunn has a good heart."

"How can you say that?" someone hollered.

"Order!" Judge McCarthy pounded his gavel.

"This is some sort of trick. You don't know anything about me," Matt said angrily.

"I know more than I want to." Mr. Stein went over and

handed Matt a piece of paper. "I received this letter from Matt
Dunn via the organ donor program. For those in the court
who don't know, Matt wanted to know who donated organs
for a transplant he had a few years back. He wanted to thank
the family of the donor. Well, you see I *do* know about your
heart, Matt, because it was given to you by my son, Michael,
the day he died. That is why I know you have a good heart,
and in Michael's memory I am going to make sure you follow
it." Mr. Stein wiped his eyes and walked out, leaving Matt Dunn
and the courtroom in stunned silence.

In view of the commotion at the hockey game and the
night, Vanessa's party had been rescheduled for the next night.
Of course, it wasn't a surprise anymore.

"Oh, thanks, Orville." I handed her the gift and she began to unwrap it.

"What did you get her?" my mom whispered. Mom was
there to chaperone me. It was kind of embarrassing, but it
was my only choice, and she was pretty cool for a mom at a
teenage party.

"I don't know what I got her." I told Mom the truth. That
afternoon I had found a note and a package from Rabbi
Spielman. The note said how he heard from Gina about my
dilemma to find the perfect gift for the perfect girl, and he
found the answer. Vanessa opened the package and said, "Oh
wow. That's beautiful. Orville, I love it." She held up a stained
glass wall ornament. It *was* beautiful. It was a scene of two

sea gulls flying over Cranberry Beach and etched in small letters in the corner was "J.S." I briefly thought of Jonah Stein and those two sea gulls, and how we were connected. The lesson Jonah and Gina were trying to teach was that we are all connected, and sometimes you have to forgive your enemies or they will eat you up. Gina knew that. Jonah learned it. They didn't let them win, and they were both free—like those sea gulls on the beach.

Vanessa hugged me and gave me a soft kiss on the cheek. "Whenever I look at this I'll think of you." I held onto her embrace. I thought it really was the perfect gift, as Kip Taylor gave me a sour look and headed for another glass of punch.

EPILOGUE

"HERE'S YOUR mail," George the mailman smiled and handed Orville Jacques' mom a handful of junk mail.

"Thanks for nothing, George," she laughed.

"I just deliver it. Good day," he laughed back.

Mrs. Jacques went into her house and leafed through it, quickly discarding the usual credit card applications, carpet cleaning coupons, and the You-have-just-won-a-million-dollars brochures. Mrs. Jacques assumed it was all junk mail, so she threw it out. But what she didn't know was that in between a flyer for a furniture store and coupons for a new pizza place, there was a postcard. It was a postcard from Ireland and it ended up thrown into the bottom of the trash by mistake. It read:

Dear Orville,

Just got to Ireland. Flight was good. Food lousy. Can't wait to meet your dad.

Sincerely,

Ivan "The Cat"

P.S. I hope I didn't hurt your neck the other night, my little mouse.

T. M. Murphy lives in Falmouth, Massachusetts. When he is not writing or cheering for the Boston Red Sox, Mr. Murphy enjoys teaching creative writing to young people. He lives and teaches his Just Write It class in a converted garage he calls The Shack.

AMY HAMILTON

Check out www.belltownmysteries.com and www.jntownsendpublishing.com.